Praise for
THE SCENT OF PINE

"Vapnyar unspools a provocative thread of suspense while charting a compelling tale of cultural displacement and yearning. . . . She writes with searing directness and immediacy, yet she seeds her prose with humor and vivid details. . . . *The Scent of Pine* shows an impressive gift, not just of language, but of insight into the human condition."

—*The Boston Globe*

"Enchanting . . . vivid and rich . . . Ms. Vapnyar has shown herself to be exquisitely sensitive to the shifting vagaries of emotion, particularly happiness. . . . Each of [her character's experiences] shimmers with possibility but also carries a creeping sense of dread, sort of like adolescent sexuality itself."

—*The New York Times*

"Vapnyar can, with a few descriptive strokes, summon images readers will feel keenly. . . . [A] book of elegant writing and propulsive storytelling."

—*Chicago Tribune*

"[A] well thought out, deeply realistic book . . . Vapnyar has created characters that readers will feel for and a story that will keep them guessing, but has done so with a sustained sense of realism that few novels ever achieve."

—bustle.com

"Vapnyar gives us a modern Scheherazade, weaving literary allusions, sexual repression and awakening . . . into a darkly funny, lonely love story evoked by the landscapes of Russia and Maine. . . . Readers of literary fiction will want to try this surprisingly quick read."

—*Booklist*

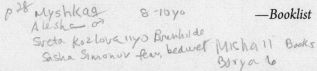

"Vapnyar's writing style feels like Lena's camp—everything seems to be in plain sight, but one can sense deeper truths hiding below the surface."

—*Kirkus Reviews*

"Lena's reminiscences vividly render the anxieties of adolescence amid the waning days of the Soviet Union."

—*Publishers Weekly*

"Like the title, promising beautiful sensations, the novel delivers a moody symphony. The characters' experience echoes Chekhov's "Lady with a Lapdog," and like Chekhov, Lara Vapnyar is an astute and loving psychologist, creating a wonderful, soul-searching, and sensual novel."

—Josip Novakovich, author of
Shopping for a Better Country and *April Fool's Day*

"Sharply observed, darkly humorous, and sexy, Vapnyar weaves her tale of midlife crisis and coming-of-age like a modern-day, Russian Scheherazade."

—Tatjana Soli, *New York Times* bestselling author of *The Lotus Eaters*

"Lara Vapnyar has always written vividly and with a droll sense of humor about personal liberty. In *The Scent of Pine*, Vapnyar takes that singular voice to a new level as she examines a singular character's release from her past and her consequential sexual liberation. *The Scent of Pine* is an important novel that questions—and miraculously answers—what it really means to be free."

—Jennifer Gilmore, author of *The Mothers* and *Something Red*

THE
SCENT
OF
PINE

Lara Vapnyar

SIMON & SCHUSTER PAPERBACKS
New York   London   Toronto   Sydney   New Delhi

Simon & Schuster Paperbacks
A Division of Simon & Schuster, Inc.
1230 Avenue of the Americas
New York, NY 10020

First Simon & Schuster trade paperback edition January 2015

SIMON & SCHUSTER PAPERBACKS and colophon are
registered trademarks of Simon & Schuster, Inc.

For information about special discounts for bulk purchases,
please contact Simon & Schuster Special Sales at
1-866-506-1949 or business@simonandschuster.com.

The Simon & Schuster Speakers Bureau can bring authors
to your live event. For more information or to book an event,
contact the Simon & Schuster Speakers Bureau at
1-866-248-3049 or visit our website at www.simonspeakers.com.

Designed by Esther Paradelo

Manufactured in the United States of America

1   3   5   7   9   10   8   6   4   2

The Library of Congress has cataloged the hardcover edition as follows:

Vapnyar, Lara, date.
The scent of pine / Lara Vapnyar. — First Simon & Schuster hardcover edition.
        pages   cm
1. College teachers—Fiction. I. Title
PS3622.A68S34 2014
813'.6—dc23   2013025893
ISBN 978-1-4767-1262-8
ISBN 978-1-4767-1263-5 (pbk)
ISBN 978-1-4767-1264-2 (ebook)

THE
SCENT
OF
PINE

ONE

It was never quiet in the woods at night. There would be a creepy rustle in the grass, or a branch would snap here or there, and that unceasing choir of cicadas. The smell was creepy too. It ought to have been some kind of romantic smell, something like pine sap heated by the sun during the day. There were plenty of pines, and it was a summer with a lot of warm, bright days, so couldn't it have smelled nice at night? But it didn't. The smell was moldy and damp and a little putrid. In daytime they could detect distinct undertones of rotten cabbage that came from the so-called Cabbage Creek, a small stream leading from the kitchen to the woods, where the kitchen guys sometimes dumped leftover cabbage soup. But at night it just smelled of decay.

Lena kept looking at their hands, bluish-white in the moonlight. Her fingers looked so thin and transparent in his. His were sturdy and warm. Yet, it was he who disappeared. Danya.

Or sometimes the story would come to her like this:

"Masturbation is very bad for boys," Yanina Ivanovna had instructed the counselors, "bad and dangerous." The head counselor went on listing the dangers: Memory loss. Impotence. Early death. Bad grades. She was a short beefy woman.

"Just tell them: 'Hands over the blankets!'"

Lena couldn't possibly tell the kids that. She would enter the boys' bedroom, sit down on the edge of the windowsill, and begin a scary bedtime story in the most boring voice she could muster, developed specially for putting the kids to sleep. The room smelled like starched linen, toothpaste, and pee—some of the boys would hide their wet underpants under the mattresses. The boys in her unit were nine to eleven years old. They looked strangely alike in the soft light coming from the moon in the window and the yellow hall lamps. Shorn hair, large ears, dark skinny necks against the heavy white pillows. Eyes closed. Eyes wide open. Eyes squinted in a giggle. Eyes clouded by tears. Hands moving under the blankets seeking out comfort and peace.

As most of the eyes closed to the sound of Lena's voice, she would walk from bed to bed moving their sticky little hands to a decent position above the blanket.

Or at other times the story would start with her friend Inka:

Inka had light brown hair streaked with pink and blue, and the longest fingernails Lena had ever seen. They shared a tiny counselors' bedroom that always smelled of Inka's face cream, her nail polish, and her hairspray. Sometimes Inka composed poems in her sleep. She would wake up in the middle of the night and yank on Lena's arm, "Lenka, listen! Listen, listen."

"What?" she would groan.

"Listen to my poem:

"'Take your bread and take your spoon.
You'll be really healthy then.'"

"That's your poem?" Lena would ask.

"Yeah, I guess it sounded much better in my sleep. I might have lost some lines."

"Inka, that's just the camp's call for dinner:

'Take your bread and take your spoon
They will serve the dinner soon.'"

"Oh, shit . . ." Inka would say, and, giggling, they would go back to sleep.

Lena's train to the conference was scheduled to depart from Penn Station at 5:40 P.M. on Wednesday. At 5:41 it started to move softly, gliding farther and farther through the tunnel. Lena stored her suitcase in the rack by the toilet and went to look for a good window seat, which wasn't that difficult since the car was mostly empty. She picked one in the middle, sat down, and unbuttoned her coat. She needed to calm down, but it was impossible. Less than an hour ago, she had run into Inka, whom she hadn't seen in almost ten years, ever since Lena and Vadim left Russia for the United States. People from the camp kept popping up here and there in the most unexpected places. Lena rarely traveled alone, but the last two times she had, she had bumped into one or another person from the camp. She wondered if anything similar ever happened to Vadim. He had never mentioned it. Sometimes Lena thought that it was she who made all these people materialize, because every time she found herself alone, she would think about the camp intensely and try to piece the story together, as if hoping that solving the mystery of what happened twenty years ago would help her solve the mystery of her present unhappiness. A ridiculous idea! It was nobody's fault that she was unhappy.

"Ticket, ma'am!" Lena opened her eyes and handed her ticket to the conductor. The looming brownstones of Washington Heights were rushing past. How she hated to be called ma'am!

Lena put the ticket stub in her breast pocket, folded her arms behind her head, and closed her eyes.

Ten years ago, she had run into the head counselor, Yanina Ivanovna, in New York, exiting a Century 21 store with her Russian tour group. She clearly didn't remember Lena, but she pretended to. And about five years ago in London, she saw one of the girls from her unit, Sveta

Kozlova, at the Royal Albert Hall of all places. Lena remembered Sveta as a tall, pudgy nine-year-old; she would never have recognized her in this six-foot-two-inch beauty. But Sveta had run up to Lena and lifted her off the ground with her hug. Sveta said that she was married to one of the richest men in Russia, who was now exiled to London. She kept insisting they all have a drink after the concert, and that she had something amazing to show Lena, but Lena developed a bad headache and had to leave before the concert was over. She didn't think she would enjoy the company of glamorous "new Russians" anyway, so she didn't regret leaving.

And now Inka. Lena had lost touch with Inka after Lena and Vadim left Russia for the U.S. years ago, but in the last few years, news of Inka had been popping up here and there. Apparently, she had become a prominent human rights activist. Her name appeared in the *New Yorker,* her opinion in the *New York Times,* a glimpse of her on CNN, her deep, lulling voice on NPR. Who would have ever believed that Inka would become famous? And as a *human rights* activist? Lena was both jealous and proud. She had the urge to boast that Inka and she used to be friends, best friends, but there was nobody besides Vadim to boast to, and Vadim hated when she talked about her experiences at the camp.

And now she had seen Inka in New York. By pure chance. Friends gave Lena a lift to the city, where she was supposed to take a train to Saratoga Springs, and since she had an hour before her train, she decided to go to Macy's. She was on the first floor smelling all those perfume sticks, getting nauseous from the stench, when she noticed a plump woman, with a long nose and messy blond hair standing at a counter nearby. The woman was wearing glasses, so it was hard to see her face, but something familiar about her carriage, about the way she moved her whole body rather than craning her neck when she tried to see something behind the counter, reminded Lena of Inka. "Inka!" she yelled, impulsively, and Inka turned, removed her glasses and squealed in delight. It turned out that Inka had come to the United States to give a series of lectures about Chechnya. When they hugged, it comforted Lena that Inka felt just as soft and pliable as she used to. They didn't have very much time to catch up, though. Lena's train was leaving in half an hour, and this was Inka's last weekend in the U.S., so they just exchanged quick essential information. Lena was surprised to learn that Inka was about to end her third marriage and Inka was even more surprised that Lena was still married to Vadim. Awkwardly, as if to make up for it, Lena began to gush about her two sons, Misha and Borya, but Inka didn't have much to add to that part of the conversation. She seemed happy to see Lena, but there was no real warmth. Inka kept fiddling with her phone, checking her messages, texting. Her long nails tapped against the keys with annoying speed. Lena asked if Inka stayed in touch with anybody else from the camp. Inka shook her head. She was too busy to keep in touch, but Sveta Kozlova had visited her recently in Moscow. "Remember Brunhilde, that fat monster? She is married to some tycoon and lives in London. We talked about how you had a secret admirer at the camp," Inka said, winking at Lena wickedly, but insisted the story was too long to tell then. She promised to tell Lena more in an email. They exchanged email addresses and phone numbers, and swore that this time they would stay in touch for sure, though Lena didn't think either of them really believed it.

Lena raised her arms above her head and stretched against the train seat. It was much more fun to think about Inka than about this stupid conference, which was making her nervous. She used to love train travel. The slight tremor in her knees, the vibration of the train, used to give her that bubbly feeling that something exciting was in store for her. These days though, premonitions like that only brought on panic. This morning, as she was boarding the bus to New York, she felt only a momentary sensation of escape, followed by exhaustion and disappointment.

She was annoyed with Inka. Her condescending "Oh!" when Lena said that she worked at a community college, her tapping fingers, but most of all her surprise that Lena was still married to Vadim. Lena used to be proud of their longevity, but recently the thought that she might stay with him forever filled her with dread. The feeling was especially intense on vacations and weekends, when they were thrown together for long stretches of time, with few distractions except their two boys, until everything—every single little thing that one of them said or did—annoyed the other to the point of violence. "Those are piling up, aren't they?" Vadim said to her last weekend, gesturing to the rather tall pile of magazines on her nightstand. He asked her to put them away. She didn't. He walked up to her nightstand and pulled a magazine from the bottom of the pile so that all the other magazines fell to the floor. She grabbed one of them and threw it at him. She hit him on the shoulder. It wasn't that bad, but the fact that she could even think of physically hurting him was sickening. Still, Inka couldn't have possibly guessed that she'd gotten to that point. So what right did Inka have to be so surprised? But then Lena was pretty sure Inka had never liked her husband.

Lena checked her watch: Vadim and the kids must be still at the airport waiting for their flight to San Diego. She dialed the number. Misha and Borya sounded very excited, as did Vadim—apparently he let them try all those crazy massage chairs at Brookstone. Did she catch a little bit of glee in his description of how much fun they were having without her or was she just being paranoid? She felt a pang of guilt for not going with them. But they were happy, they were fine, and she was just going to a conference, which was supposed to advance her career. Why then did it feel as if she was running away?

The conductor announced the Tarrytown stop and the train came to a halt. An old woman with a gleaming leather suitcase climbed in, waddled to her seat, asked a young man to hoist the suitcase up, sat down, thanked the young man, and immediately started a lively conversation with him. Lena felt pathetic for sitting there talking to herself. She looked in her bag. It held a book, an apple, and her paper for the conference. She took out the paper, but the thought of reading it made her nervous. The conference was a big multidisciplinary event, "The Aesthetics of Oppression." A lot of big names. Historians. Writers. Architects. Even a composer who had written an opera based on the Kinsey Reports. Lena's talk, titled "Sex Education in the Former Soviet Union," had been added at the last moment, apparently after somebody else had canceled. Secretly, Lena was worried that neither she—a mere adjunct at a community college—nor her work was important enough. Vadim's reaction when she got the invitation only fed her doubts. He suggested that she had to have been a replacement. "You don't seriously believe that they'd want you?" he said. He claimed he was only providing perspective, protecting her from disappointment. And he did believe that he was acting in her best interest, she knew that. It was just that in this uncertain period in her life, when she felt like such a failure, the last thing she needed was sober perspective. The format of the talk seemed especially frightening. She would have to sit onstage with a moderator and answer her questions. Lena would have preferred a panel, so that other panelists could share the burden. Nervously, she reached into her bag for the apple but realized that she didn't want it.

In the restaurant car she bought a cup of tea and sat by a huge window with a view of the Hudson. The weak tepid tea matched the dullness of the landscape. Her mind kept returning to her encounter with Inka. Had Inka looked at her with *compassion*?

The first time Lena had met Inka, they were standing in the crowd of students waiting for the train at a station in the southeast tip of Moscow. They were all freshmen from the State Pedagogical University—on their way to the summer camp, where they would have to complete their six-week-long pedagogical practice.

Other girls stood in pairs, or in groups of three or four. Lena stood alone, thinking how for the whole nine months at the university she had failed to make a single friend. She ended up spending every recess in the bathroom, going in and out of the stalls, washing her hands until they stank of school soap, endlessly fixing her hair in front of the mirror, studying her wary face in the background of chipped tiles, blue stalls, and other girls going in and out, chatting with one another. Lena had accepted the fact that she had been unpopular in school—all that history of baking mud pies in the corner while other kids chased each other in kindergarten, or hiding behind a tree to read a book on school camping trips, or standing by the wall all alone at school dances, which could be a result of baking mud pies as a child, and hiding behind the trees as a teen. She was hoping to reverse that in college, to become, if not popular, then at least likable. Her plan had been to approach people with a smile, listen to conversations with interest, and join whatever activities they offered. None of that worked. The other students seemed to have a similar plan, but they were better and quicker at it. They formed groups of friends in a matter of days, or hours, and there was no place for Lena. Lena felt particularly excluded, because her entering college coincided with the most exciting period in all Soviet history, perestroika. It was hugely exhilarating. New things that had been previously taboo, new activities, new life. All of that created enormous pressure to be a part of something important, to be enthusiastic, energized, and active.

There was only one other person at the train stop who stood alone the way Lena did. A tall, chubby girl who was peering into a book that she held very high, very close to her face. Lena remembered that she had seen this girl in the lecture halls, and in the cafeteria, and sometimes by the window in the lobby. She was always alone and always with a book.

When the train pulled close to the stop, the tall girl shut her book and walked up to Lena and introduced herself as Inka. "Your name's Lena, right?" Lena nodded. They took seats together.

As the train passed through the ugly industrial outskirts of Moscow, Inka admitted to Lena that she hated their school and hated the idea of being a teacher. She confessed she had picked this program because it was reasonably easy to get into, and she really wanted to get out of her hometown and live in Moscow. And Lena told her that she ended up in State Pedagogical—her safety school—because she failed the auditions in the four acting schools to which she'd applied. "Acting?" Inka asked. "But you're so shy." Lena explained that acting allowed people to become somebody they were not, even if only for a brief time. She wouldn't be shy on stage. She said that she wanted to be an actress because she really wanted to live many lives instead of just one. She wanted to see what it was like to murder somebody, or to be murdered, what it was like to be at war, to live in the nineteenth century, to lose a loved one, but she didn't want the experience to affect the rest of her life. As she spoke, Lena was scared that Inka would laugh at her, but Inka didn't laugh. Instead, seeing how embarrassed Lena was, she confessed that she composed poems in her sleep. Lena felt a kind of affection blossoming, not because the other girl wrote poems, but because she'd been willing to reveal it to Lena to ease her embarrassment.

Inka had light brown hair streaked with pink and blue. She dressed differently from other girls in their school too—most of the clothes that she wore were imported and obviously expensive, but they seemed to be bought at random, so they didn't match, and some of them didn't even fit. On the train Inka said that she'd come to Moscow from a small town and was under the impression that Muscovites existed on a different frequency, which she couldn't tune in to. That was her excuse for why she couldn't make friends. Lena couldn't respond, having been born and raised in Moscow. If she couldn't make friends, it was only because she sucked at making friends, or simply because she sucked.

As the train got farther from Moscow, Inka asked Lena if she had a boyfriend. Lena shook her head. "Me neither," Inka said, explaining that she had gone out with plenty of boys, but there hadn't been anybody to really spark her interest.

Lena was terrified that the next question would be whether she had had sex, so she decided to change the subject.

"What have you got there?" she asked, pointing at the box with books Inka was holding in her lap. Inka opened the top of the crate and showed her.

The Satiricon, The Golden Ass, The Canterbury Tales, The Decameron, The Arabian Nights, and *Excerpts from the Bible* with the long introduction meant to prove how wrong and silly the Bible was, written by somebody who had a Ph.D. in scientific atheism.

All the books were from the summer list for their Foreign Literature Part 1 class. Lena laughed—she had the same books in her backpack.

Plus, she had several issues of *Art of Cinema* magazine, with the screen-play of *Last Tango in Paris* in the last one. "Ooh! That's the one where he—never mind—I'll have to borrow that!" Inka said.

About two hours into the trip, when the train was passing some bleak countryside, with lopsided barns and skinny cows stuck in mud, they unwrapped and ate omelet sandwiches that Lena's mother had made for her, and little meat pies that Inka's mother had baked at home and brought to Moscow on a train, in a big aluminum pot wrapped in a woolen shawl.

Inka said that her mother was only thirty-four years old. She got pregnant with Inka while still in high school and had to marry Inka's father. Her father was a smart, mean man who had once been an artist but was now just a common drunk. Her mother was a hairdresser and very pretty. Her biggest fear was that Inka would get pregnant and have to get married young too. Inka had to promise her mother that what-ever happened she wouldn't get married before she was twenty-three.

"Why twenty-three?" Lena asked.

Inka didn't know. She sighed and cleaned a spot on the window with her sleeve. She said that her biggest wish was to escape the pattern. She said that it was the scariest thing—falling into a pattern and knowing what was going to happen to you.

Lena's parents had gotten divorced when she turned sixteen. The official version was that her mother threw her father out. At first her mother was euphoric, energized, proud of her resolve. She was brim-ming with plans for her new independent life, but in a month or two she started to fall apart. What horrified Lena the most was her mother's staggering insecurity. She acquired this strange new expression, this sideways questioning look, as if she suspected that people were laugh-ing at her. But if she told a joke, it was the other way around; she was terrified that people wouldn't laugh, and she smiled with such gratitude when they did. And even those stupid omelet sandwiches that she'd been proudly making for years: Now she would push the omelet from the pan onto the cutting board and freeze with the knife suspended in her fingers: "Do you even like them? Are they even good? Lena, please tell me the truth, do you like my omelet sandwiches?" Lena couldn't stand her like that. She couldn't bear to talk to her, to look at her. She tried to hide from her mother's unhappiness as if it were an infectious disease. She loathed herself for that, but she couldn't help it. Her father, on the other hand, seemed to be okay. "I feel as if I were learning to breathe anew," he'd whispered when Lena saw him last. He rented a tiny room in a shoddy, crowded, roach-infested apartment, but he didn't seem to mind. He began to wear a look of cautious happiness, as if he'd discovered a treasure and was afraid that someone would take it away. Lena couldn't bear to see him happy, when she knew how much the divorce pained her mother. She couldn't bring herself to visit him after that. She cried at night, both hating and missing him.

Lena looked at Inka's solemn profile, which didn't go with the mess of pink and blue in her hair, and wondered if she could understand. She looked like she could.

About an hour away from the camp, the scenery changed dramatically. Woods gradually supplanted fields and meadows, and the closer we got to the camp, the denser the woods became. Inka and Lena stopped talking and looked out the window. At one point they thought they saw a moose. The girls in the seat behind them giggled in delight.

"Was it a moose?" one of them asked.

"I think so, I saw a few last year," another said, launching into stories about her superfun experience at the camp the year before. Fresh air, sunbathing, good food, plenty of free time. Not only that, but the camp belonged to the Ministry of Defense, so many, many guys worked there. Officers. Soldiers drafted into the Soviet Army from college. Some were even seriously smart. She gushed about discothèques under a starry sky, the riverbank where you could take romantic walks, and the touchingly beautiful clearings in the woods where the grass was tall and silky-soft under your back.

Inka and Lena exchanged glances and smiled. Inka said that she had thought she'd fall in love when she started college. "It's been eight months—and nothing. Eight months!" Her face tensed with panic. Lena knew exactly how she felt. She told Inka that she had been playing the "boyfriend game" for several years herself. Every time she was about to reach a certain milestone—turn fifteen, sixteen, enter high school, college—she thought, "Now!" And nothing happened. Every time she was going to someplace new—on vacation, on a long train trip, to a party, to a museum—she thought, "There!" And nothing. She would meet a boy from time to time, and he would ask her out, and she would feel a surge of excitement, but the excitement would evaporate pretty soon—usually before the date ended.

In three hours, when they finally got off the train, their knees were trembling and their butts hurt from all the riding. They felt queasy and lightheaded, but they were immediately taken in by the beauty. It was very quiet and unusually cold for July. Everything had the air of spring. The woods, the pines, the squishy soil under their feet, the unbelievably loud singing of birds. Inka shivered in her light shirt and laughed. Lena laughed too. They wanted to run, to squeal, to jump. On the way to the camp headquarters, they passed a group of soldiers sawing branches off a huge fallen pine. One of them waved. They waved back. Lena was overcome with the strange feeling that she experienced only a couple of times after that. She didn't know what to call it. Anticipation of happiness? No, it had to be stronger than that. Certainty of happiness.

Inevitability of happiness.

The train arrived at Saratoga Springs at a quarter to ten. There were no taxis at the station. The thin crowd that got off the train with Lena petered out within minutes. Some people walked to cars that had been waiting for them with their lights on, others disappeared along the semidark streets leading to the town. And now Lena stood all alone facing the dark parking lot with the empty, brightly lit station behind her. She walked back into the station and asked the woman at the ticket booth for the number of the car service. The woman gave her the number but said that the hotel was only fifteen minutes away by foot. "Twenty—max," she added before dropping her glazed stare back to her Stephen King novel.

It was slightly colder here than it had been in Boston. Streetlights and windows of the closed shops shone brightly, brighter than necessary, Lena thought. She would see her shadow against the wall of one or another strange house. The shadow would be larger than life, and sometimes if the light was especially bright, the shadow would be so large that she saw the contours of her head looming on somebody's roof. There were no people around. No movement—not even wind. And no sounds, except for the pleasant rapping of her heels against the pavement. She would hear an occasional car honk up on the main street, too far in the distance to sound real. There was nothing specifically American about this place. A town like this could be anywhere. Western Europe. Eastern Europe. Russia. Lena had a fleeting thought that her summer camp memories had actually transported her to Russia.

It took her thirty minutes to get to the hotel, and by the time they gave her the keys, it was ten fifty-five. She went up to her room and dialed Vadim's number. He said that he was okay as were the kids. He asked if she was okay. She said that she was. They didn't know what else to say to each other. Lena plopped down onto the bed, feeling tired and heavy, as if the bed was pressing down on her and not vice versa.

Impossibility of happiness was what she felt now.

Two

The hotel pool was small and plain, functional—no mosaic or exotic plants. Saturated with morning light. Empty, except for a teenage boy who was folding towels. Lena had been swimming the length of the pool back and forth hoping that it would relax her before the talk. So far, it hadn't.

She found the slippery heaviness of the water around her body annoying, and the insufficient length of the pool bored her—it was an effort to turn back and continue every time she touched a wall.

The steamed-up door opened with a deep sigh, releasing a thin trail of cold air. A man in a white bathrobe walked in and headed toward the deep end of the pool. He stopped by the chair where Lena had dropped her bathrobe and took off his own, placing it on the adjacent chair. He looked at Lena and made a hesitant movement toward the pool. He appeared to be feeling like an intruder. He was tall, a little slouchy, with stooped shoulders and strong calves. He looked at Lena with dark sunken eyes, an intense stare that made her look away. He jumped in with a modest splash and took the right lane. Lena switched from the middle lane to the left. For a few minutes they swam parallel to each other, in different directions—he, underwater, fast—she, on the surface, slowly, on her back, then on her stomach.

The pool was so small that there was something intimate about the experience, awkwardly stirring, almost indecent. Lena thought that she'd better get out. She climbed out of the pool, walked to her chair, put on her flip-flops, picked up her bathrobe, and headed toward the door. The man swam to the edge and pulled himself up. He looked as if he was about to say something, but then changed his mind and dove in.

At 9 o'clock, Lena found her way to the main building where the lectures were taking place. The room that was assigned for Lena's talk was a large lovely room, with big windows, and two green armchairs on a stage. Though the talk was supposed to start in five minutes, there was nobody there. She sat down in one of the two armchairs and waited, with her paper on her lap. Across the hall from her room was the breakfast lounge. The smell of fresh coffee wafted in, and she watched the waiters pass her door with trays of colorful fruit and baskets of gleaming bagels. Since it looked like she had some time before she'd have to begin her talk, Lena was tempted to run across the hall to pick up a bagel or a piece of fruit but knew she'd be too nervous to eat anyway.

At about 9:25 the moderator popped in and said that she shouldn't worry, people were often late for morning events. Lena waited. Nobody came. A blond woman with a long nose and long loose hair peeked in, looked at Lena, and walked away. Lena stood up and walked to the back of the room so that nobody else who happened to peek in would guess that she was a lonely presenter.

At 9:35 the moderator came back, sat down in the back row next to Lena, and made an attempt at conversation.

"Sleepyheads, huh?" she said.

Lena nodded.

The attempt at conversation failed.

The moderator looked at her watch, sighed, and stood up. She shook Lena's hand and said how sorry she was.

Lena went back to the breakfast room, completely empty now, littered with stained coffee cups and half-eaten bagels, with overflowing trash containers. She ate a little of everything that was left on the trays, then some more of everything, took a cup of coffee and went outside.

She sat down on a bench surrounded by flowerless lilacs—it must have been pretty a couple of weeks ago—and dialed Vadim's number, wondering if he'd be awake. He was. He asked about her talk. Lena said that it had gone fine, better than she'd expected. Nice crowd, interesting questions. She didn't feel like telling the truth, yet lying left her feeling a little angry, not with herself but with Vadim for some reason.

Lena contemplated whether she could skip the rest of the conference, pack her things and go, but instead she plunged into the masochism of walking down the corridor and listening to the sounds of laughter and applause coming from other rooms. Back in Russia, she used to imagine America as something like this campus—a country with many buildings and many paths leading from building to building, a building with many rooms and many corridors leading from room to room. Nobody came to her room. Nobody cared to listen to her. And yet other rooms were filled with people and voices and laughter. Speakers spoke, listeners reacted to what they said. As if everyone around her was engaging in some sort of a chemical reaction, from which she was excluded. Lena was suddenly seized by an acute feeling of being a stranger in America.

She'd lived here for thirteen years, and in that time her relationship with her adoptive country had gone through several stages. Originally, she had imagined America as a land steeped in adventure, which filled her with panicky adoration. Then there was the incomprehension and dejection which characterized her first months in America, when everything had seemed so strange and hostile: the scenery, the climate, the people. Mostly the people. Everybody seemed to participate in a complicated game based on very particular rules. But eventually, she stopped looking at Americans as a unified mass. They were all lonely to a certain degree, they were all strangers to a certain degree. Some were accessible, others were not; some were interested in her, others were not. This led her to an acceptance of America and Americans that she had enjoyed for the last few years. But recently, with her career going nowhere and her loneliness getting greater and greater, she'd started to feel the onset of panic again.

She read off the titles of presentations printed on little sheets of paper and clipped to the doors, marveling at how stupid they sounded and how transparent their metaphors were. "Closed In." "Stilted Bodies. Stilted Souls." "The Magic of Prison States." Yet, people laughed and applauded. Lena caught the word "masturbation" as she was passing "The Magic of Prison States," and she stopped by the open door to listen. She had thought the speaker used "masturbation" as some kind of metaphor, but no, it turned out he meant it in the literal sense. He was talking about graphic novels set in oppressive societies. The speaker had a soft, pleasant voice, a calm and confident manner. Not a trace of an accent. He had no business talking about prison states. What could he possibly know? There were notes of warm amusement in his tone that suggested that he understood whatever there was to understand about it. She had lived in America for thirteen years, and she didn't understand it at all. Where did this arrogance come from? Holding the door, she peeked into the room. The speaker was a tall man with stooped shoulders, restless, a little awkward, seemingly too aware of the impression he was making. Lena couldn't see his face. There were just a few people in the audience. Six. No, seven—an old man slumped by the window. He looked like he was asleep. Lena heard notes of anxiety in the speaker's voice that she hadn't caught before. She felt something like compassion for him. As she leaned against it, the door made a screech, and the man turned toward her. Lena recognized him right away. The fact that he had caught her eavesdropping combined with the fact that he had seen her in the intimacy of the pool made her intensely embarrassed. Lena walked from the room.

The stinky, squeaky floors of the hall made her cringe. The linoleum was a frightening canary-yellow, with a pattern that reminded her of the floor in the camp headquarters where they had their weekly meetings with Yanina. Black swirly lines and brown specks. Lena had been so frightened of Yanina that she would sit staring at the pattern on the floor the whole time.

///////////////////////

At the first meeting there were tea and sandwiches. They entered a square room with tables and chairs and two soldiers in the corner pouring the tea from a big vat into thick glasses. The tea was for them, as were cheese sandwiches on a big tray. "Help yourself!" one of the soldiers said. He had brown squinty eyes that seemed to say: "Girls! You don't know how lucky you are."

Some women were sitting on the chairs by the wall. One said that she was the camp nurse; another said that she was in charge of the supplies. Natasha. Galina. Nadezhda. Svetlana. Zhenya. Lena forgot which was which right away. She felt as if they were in a theater, the play was about to start, and the actors were already on the stage, but they didn't know who among them would be the principals and who would be mere extras.

A girl next to Lena whispered: "Thank God, Vedenej isn't here!" Lena asked who that was. "Major Vedeneev, the camp director. Everybody calls him Vedenej."

Yanina walked into the room and didn't take a sandwich. In retrospect, this was the first thing that had alarmed Lena about Yanina. The other woman took a chair and moved it away from the table to the middle of the room. She sat down, her thick legs wide-set and firmly planted on the floor. She looked the girls over, one by one. She seemed to be studying them, even testing them with her stare.

Lena had put her glass down when Yanina walked in, but she didn't know what to do with the big piece of crust left from her sandwich. She couldn't finish it—everybody else had stopped eating, and she didn't want to leave it on a table—she didn't want anybody, especially Yanina, to think that she was so spoiled that she didn't eat crust. So she just sat there with the piece of crust clutched in her hand.

Then Yanina started to talk. Her face was meaty and red—her cheeks, her chin, her nose, her forehead, even her ears. Her thin yellow eyebrows looked indecent and scary against all that red, which became deeper and deeper as she talked. Lena decided that it would be safer to stare at the floor. Yanina's voice was low and sharp, and she seemed to hammer her sentences right into their heads.

"If the property of a unit gets stolen or lost—you're responsible. If a kid gets sick with food poisoning—you're responsible. If a kid gets lost in the woods—you're responsible. If a kid from our unit falls and breaks his neck—you're responsible. If something bad did happen, in the best-case scenario, your college would be notified and you would have a bad record forever, and in the worst-case scenario you would go to prison.

"By the way, are you aware of the dangers of masturbation?"

In 1989, perestroika, and the sexual revolution, had yet to reach summer camps and pedagogical colleges.

Yanina proceeded to give the girls a lecture on how hormones were our worst enemies, and how all sexual evil started with hands under the blankets and gradually led to rape and pregnancies, and how almost every camp had some incidents every year. And how it was the counselors' responsibility if anything like that happened here.

The schedule and the long list of our specific tasks followed—everybody was too stunned and intimidated to listen properly—and then Yanina announced that each unit would be assigned to two counselors, and they could choose the age of the children.

"We'll take the littlest! The littlest!" Inka yelled before Yanina even finished her sentence. The girl who sat next to Lena whispered to her that "the littlest" were the most work, but it was too late.

After Yanina assigned the rest of the units and dismissed the girls, one of the women, either Zhenya or Natasha, asked if Major Vedeneev was going to greet the girls, but Yanina waved her hand. "He will greet the girls some other time," she said.

Lena's head was spinning as the girls walked out of the room one by one, clutching the typed papers with the daily schedule and the kids' names. She felt as if she was about to faint. She was sure that every single horrible thing that Yanina mentioned was bound to happen, and that she and Inka would be severely punished. She turned to Inka, hoping that she'd reassure her and maybe even mock her for her fears, but Inka looked just as scared. After the meeting they went into their unit, found the tiny room designated for counselors, and started to unpack. Lena felt uneasy taking her clothes out in front of Inka, because she was afraid that they would somehow give away the fact that she was a virgin. She decided to leave them in the suitcase, and pushed the suitcase under her bed. Inka looked at her and shrugged. She must have thought that Lena was a slob. But being considered a slob was so much better than being considered a virgin. Inka proceeded to hang some of her clothes on hangers and put others in drawers. Her clothes looked very serious and adult-like. Blouses. Skirts. Sundress. More blouses. White panties. Flowery panties. Whoa! Huge bra! Bigger than Lena's mother's. She then filled her nightstand with all kinds of bottles, and jars, and containers of hair spray and deodorant, and huge curlers and hairbrushes. All the jars were closed, but a sweet chemical smell filled the room. Inka plopped onto her bed, stretched, and scratched one foot with the other.

THREE

The conference reception attracted Lena with all its busy noise and hectic movement. She felt entertained for a minute or two, watching all those people, choosing food to put on her plate, enjoying the sweet chill of Riesling on her tongue, and half-listening to the merged-together buzz of the conversations.

Lena was momentarily seized by a powerful desire to be noticed. To be admired? Maybe, she wasn't sure. But she needed to be seen, to make an impression, to be on the receiving end of some interest, curiosity, attention. The hunger that she felt was almost physical. She looked around, hoping that she'd see the man from the pool. He wasn't there. She scanned the room trying to find faces familiar from the conference brochure. There was Althea LaGrange from Tufts. Lizzie Gess from Wellesley. Gerry Baumann from Harvard. Gerry Baumann was a Pulitzer Prize winner, so his picture had been the largest. A fat, balding man with a splotchy face, he looked restless and tense. Lena could hardly imagine initiating small talk with anybody, let alone with somebody like that. Althea LaGrange didn't seem any more accessible. Lena was becoming increasingly aware of how awkward it must have seemed moving through the room completely alone, without direction or purpose. Anybody who bothered to look at her would have noticed this and the fact that she had an embarrassing amount of food on her plate. So, she retreated onto the porch and stood there sipping her wine, balancing her plate on the banister, trying to tell herself that she was just fine here, restless, alone, but with a pile of shrimp on her plate.

Somebody cleared his throat.

"You picked the best spot!"

Lena turned and saw the man from the pool.

"Yes, it's quiet here."

"Didn't I see you earlier today at the pool?"

"Yes," she said. "I think so."

The man had longish graying hair that would have looked pretentious if it hadn't been a little unkempt. She found him slightly pathetic and this fueled her confidence.

"So," he said, "are you enjoying the conference?"

"No," Lena said, surprising herself with her frankness, "not at all. Nobody came to my talk today. Not a soul."

Strangely, she felt better as soon as she admitted that, but the man looked concerned.

"What was your topic?"

"Sexual education in Soviet Russia."

"Sounds amazing. I would've come."

"Thank you."

"My name is Ben, by the way."

"Lena."

His eyes were really very dark.

"So tell me, Lena, do you teach sexual education?"

She laughed.

"No, I teach film history. You?"

"History of the graphic novel at Rutgers. Do you like graphic novels?"

"I don't know. Probably not. I haven't read that many."

Actually, she hadn't read any, but she didn't want to admit that.

"Tell me about your presentation. What were you planning to talk about?"

He appeared to be genuinely interested.

"Well, how sexual education was mostly prohibiting things rather than informing."

"Tell me more!"

Lena smiled.

"For example, this: I worked in a Russian summer camp once, where the head counselor insisted that the kids sleep with their hands over the blankets."

"You were a counselor?"

"Yes. I was eighteen."

"How could you possibly ensure 'hands over the blankets'?"

"The head counselor suggested that we simply yell at the kids, but our more humane idea was to tell the kids stories until they fell asleep. Horror stories worked best, because the kids were so scared that they weren't about to do anything under the blankets."

"Horror stories? How's that more humane?"

"You see, my co-counselor Inka dug out this article in *Psychology Today* that said that horror stories were very healthy, because imaginary horrors managed to distract us from whatever real fears we had, and calm us down. Neither Inka nor I had been to summer camp as children, so we didn't know any of the classic horror stories. And that's where our college summer reading list came in handy. *The Arabian Nights, Canterbury Tales, Decameron, Divine Comedy*. We would recount kid-sized renditions of the stories until the kids fell asleep."

"What would a kid-sized *Divine Comedy* sound like?"

"It wasn't mine. It was Inka's. It went something like this:

"'Yeah, well, I have to tell you, kids, Hell wasn't a nice place at all. They hit people there and even roasted them in the fire.'

"And the kids would ask 'Like we do with potatoes?'

"'Uh-huh. Exactly like that. Now imagine that you are that potato.'"

"You were horrible!"

"I know!"

"What about *The Decameron*?"

"'Once upon a time, in Florence, which is this really cute city in Italy, which used to be like a whole separate country, there was an epidemic of plague.'

"And the kids would ask 'What's plague?'

"'Plague, you know, it's like flu, only much worse. You catch it if you don't wash your hands or brush your teeth. You develop these scary enormous boils all over your body and then you die. So these people in Florence didn't like to wash their hands, and they all got sick.'"

"Poor kids! But you know what, it sounds a little familiar. A summer camp, where counselors stopped children masturbating by scaring them to death. I might have read a book about that."

"I don't think so. I honestly doubt that anybody else would think of that. But the kids loved our stories. They kept asking for more."

A waiter with a tray full of dirty glasses opened the door, gave them a look and went back.

"I think the dinner's over," Lena said, heading toward the door to the reception lounge.

When they walked back into the room, only a few people were left in the corner, eating cake off tiny round plates and drinking coffee from the same institutional mugs they laid out at breakfast. The waiters were removing warming trays with the remains of lasagna and couscous. The trash bins overflowed with paper plates, glasses stained with red wine, forks, and half-eaten rolls. Lena slipped on a piece of melon somebody had dropped. Ben reached for her, but she grabbed the edge of the table instead.

They both stopped at the door. She didn't want this to be over. She had gotten her wish. Somebody had noticed her, had listened to her, been interested in her. She had forgotten how good that felt! But instead of quenching it, this encounter seemed to intensify her hunger. She didn't want to have an affair. She could swear that she didn't. She just wanted the attention, the sweet wonderful undivided attention. Lena hoped Ben would offer to continue the conversation. Ask her to a bar? It wasn't that late yet.

"Listen," he said, "do you have your conference paper with you?"

Her conference paper?

"My conference paper? Yes, it's in my room, why?"

"Would you let me read it? I'm fascinated by the subject."

Lena summoned the paper in her head, trying to decide if it was good enough to show to Ben. Was it too boring? Too poorly written? No, it wasn't. It wasn't brilliant, but it was okay. Peppered with subtle humor. She hoped Ben would be able to appreciate that. She imagined Ben reading it in his hotel room, leafing through the pages, smiling at her jokes, thinking about their meeting, remembering her face, the sound of her voice. The thought filled her with strange excitement.

"Okay," Lena said. "If you really want to see it."

"I do."

They walked down the narrow path through the park on the way back to the hotel. Towering trees whose leaves rustled high above their heads. Occasional benches—some of them missing planks in the middle. Lena wished desperately for Ben to touch her, to take her hand, or put his arm around her shoulders, or just brush his fingers against her back, but he walked with his hands in the pockets of his jacket. Dim streetlights a little too yellow. There were no stars in the sky, just the occasional bright spark of a plane, and the half-moon in a pale halo.

When they arrived at the lobby of the hotel, however, it was so brightly lit by contrast that Lena felt like closing her eyes for a moment.

"Will you wait for me?" Lena asked Ben. "I'll be right down with my paper."

There was loud piano music coming from the bar, and he had to lean closer and ask her to repeat. His heated breath on her skin made Lena dizzy. She repeated her question.

"Sure," he said. "I'll be at the bar."

Upstairs, Lena gave her paper a quick once-over. There was a typo on page 3. A long winding paragraph on page 6. A stupid joke and two more typos on page 7. Lena knew that the quality of her paper didn't matter, but by the time she made it to the bar, she was sick with anxiety.

She couldn't find Ben right away. She finally spotted him at the back of the bar, sitting across from the fat red-faced man whom she recognized as Gerry Baumann. Lena smiled and waved at Ben, but Ben shot her a pleading look and shook his head. She stopped. Gerry's meaty hand was now on Ben's sleeve. He was kneading Ben's arm and pushing him down toward his bar table.

"So, how's our little Leslie, Ben? Are you treating her well?"

"She's fine, Gerry."

"Glad to hear that. When is your wedding, then? Are you planning on inviting me? Wouldn't it be monstrous if you didn't?"

Lena turned and walked toward the elevator. As the elevator doors closed, she saw Ben desperately looking in her direction.

Up in her room, Lena shoved her paper back into her bag, changed into her nightgown and plopped onto the bed. She couldn't believe how upset she was.

There was a missed call from Vadim on her phone. Lena dialed his number, but he couldn't talk because he was busy with his parents, and she felt relieved that she didn't have to talk to him, and spoke instead to her children. Her six-year-old Borya asked if he could bring back a lizard from California. He was pretty sure he could catch one, they were really fast, but you could catch them while they were eating a piece of banana, he would've caught one today if he'd had something to put it in, he would go back with a paper cup tomorrow. Her eleven-year-old Misha didn't know what to say—like Lena, he was never any good on the phone. He must be lonely there; she had the feeling that the intensity of his California relatives frightened him. She imagined him hiding out in one of the empty rooms—her in-laws had a huge sprawling house—with a book or a videogame, lying on his stomach on the bed, propped on his elbows, feet in the air. Thin legs sporting white socks. The socks must be dirty by now. And Borya, who was healthy and square, built more like his father, would be running around the house looking for his brother. He was so cheerful and lively all the time, but what if he felt lonely too? She felt an urge to hug them both. To protect them, to be protected by them. It was strange how affection and pity went hand in hand. How, whenever she felt true affection, her heart would ache with compassion, even when there was no obvious reason for it. She'd learned that while dealing with the children at camp, though it had taken her a while.

At first Lena didn't even see the kids as human beings with their own feelings, fears, and problems. She thought of them as creatures specially designed to provide counselors with work and to create problems that would get them all punished.

As they waited for the kids to arrive, Lena kept checking her watch and silently praying that maybe they wouldn't come at all, that maybe a war would start, or a sudden epidemic of plague, or a nearby nuclear plant would explode, and the camp would be canceled before she started to work there. And then, an hour later, the buses started rolling in, sending clouds of dust into the air. One, two, three, four . . . "You go meet bus number eight, your kids are in there," somebody told them. The doors opened and, one by one, the kids started to get out. Little kids between the ages of eight and ten, smaller than Lena'd expected, wearing shorts and dusty sandals and summer hats, carrying their labeled suitcases, tired after a two-hour bus ride, terrified of the camp, terrified of the counselors, terrified of each other, some restless, some looking as if they hadn't woken up yet, some crying because they had been tortured by bullies during the ride, some crying because they were already missing their mothers, some crying for no reason at all. Lena realized, with a start, that she had no idea how to deal with children. She was supposed to tell them what to do, and they were supposed to listen. But what if they wouldn't? And then she heard Inka's voice: "Okay now, kids! Pick up your things and let's go to our building. Go!" Lena could hear an unmistakable note of fear in her voice. Lena had read somewhere that dogs could always feel your fear and that they would tear you apart when they did, but kids apparently didn't work that way. They picked up their things and followed Inka.

The first few days swirled by in a nonstop storm of big and small tasks. Wake the kids, take them to the bathroom, yell at them so they wouldn't splash each other, search for missing toothbrushes, search for toilet paper, chase a slippery piece of soap on the floor, yell at the kids some more, take them back to the bedrooms to dress, search for missing socks, search for missing pants—how can you lose your pants?! Help them make the beds, look for missing sheets—how can a sheet go missing?! Take the kids to assembly, make sure the kids stand straight and don't talk, hiss at them since yelling is not permitted during the morning assembly. Take them to breakfast, distribute the bread and butter cut into little cubes, have thirty seconds of peace while gulping down some tasteless kasha with a cup of weak tepid coffee, yell at the kids who smeared butter on their chairs, at those who smeared butter on their knees, and especially at those who threw butter cubes at one another, yell at the kids who don't want to finish their kasha, yell at the kids who finish too soon and are now bothering other kids. By the time they took the kids for the scheduled three hours of playing outside, Lena and Inka could no longer yell. They would just yank them by their sleeves or grab them by the collars of their shirt if they started to fight or tried to run too far.

But what got to Lena the most was the constant counting. Counting the kids before going to breakfast, during breakfast, after breakfast, before letting them play outside, as they played outside.

What soldiers? What romantic walks? The whole universe seemed to shrink. The geography became limited to the distance from their unit to the cafeteria, from their unit to the club, from the club to the headquarters. The complex system of sensations and emotions that Lena had possessed before was reduced to just two: anxiety and exhaustion. The world of numbers shrunk to 29—the number of children in their unit. Lena could barely distinguish between them, except for those who gave them the most trouble. They were the only ones whose names she still remembered.

There was Myshka (Katya Myshkina), a mousy little girl with a creepy fondness for older men. Whenever she saw a soldier walk past, she would run after him and try to hug him or offer him candy. She and Inka had to keep an eye on her at all times. Alesha was a blond, sweet-looking suck-up who could suddenly turn into this screeching, red-faced little devil, ready to kick, hit, crush anything he could get his hands on. You couldn't reason with him, or yell at him, but he did yield to physical strength. Sveta Kozlova, on the other hand, was only eleven but already as tall as Lena, and thicker than she was. Sveta had no qualms about hitting a counselor, which she demonstrated with Inka, or even squeezing a counselor and lifting her off the ground, which she demonstrated with Lena. Inka called her Brunhilde. The only way to control her was to appeal to the kindness of her heart. "Sveta, please, I know you can do whatever you want, but I'm going to be in so much trouble if you're not there for the morning assembly." Sometimes it worked, sometimes it didn't. Still, the worst one was Sasha Simonov. Most of the time, he seemed to be pretty harmless, a scrawny, quiet kid who loved to draw. He usually sat peacefully in a corner somewhere with his notebook and crayons, until his inner demon took hold of him and he would start crying and sobbing, and eventually have a vomiting fit. Plus, he wouldn't sleep at night. His eyes stayed wide open and Lena could see the horror in there, so much horror that it gave her goose bumps. He couldn't be comforted—he was too afraid of "where he was going when he fell asleep." He stayed awake long after the other kids fell asleep, with his hands buried under the folds of his blanket. When he woke up, there would be a wet spot on his bed that went all the way to the mattress.

"Just imagine how happy his mother was to get rid of him," Inka said every time they had to turn his mattress over.

Back then, Lena was sure she would never be a mother. That she was unfit to be a mother. Even now, she had her doubts. She loved her children, there was no doubt about that, but they couldn't make her happy. And if she were a truly good, devoted mother, shouldn't the children be enough to make her happy, or at least contented?

She sighed and turned to the bleak hotel wall, hoping for a sound, solid sleep, so solid there would be no place for guilt and disappointment to creep in.

Four

The next morning Lena overslept. There were two conference panels that she needed to attend. She dressed, packed her things so she could leave for the station right after the events, and rushed downstairs to get to the campus. There was no time for a proper breakfast, so she grabbed a bagel and nibbled on it as she sat through the first panel. The discussion was on the Kinsey Reports. Lena expected it to be interesting but found it hard to concentrate. The bagel tasted like old chewing gum. The sandwich that she had during lunch break didn't taste much better. Lena dreaded seeing Ben in the cafeteria, imagining how awkward their conversation would be after he had waved her away at the bar the night before, but when she saw that Ben wasn't there, she felt something like disappointment.

By the time she got to the station, it had started to rain.

On the platform, people were shaking their umbrellas, shuffling their luggage, craning their necks to see if the train was coming.

Lena closed her umbrella and sat down on one of the benches.

She dialed Vadim's number. He said there was nothing to report. She didn't have anything to report either. She felt guilty about her encounter with Ben. Not just guilty but pathetic, because the only thing she could be guilty of was her desire to be guilty. The train heading up to

Montreal arrived on the opposite platform. Two or three people walked toward the doors. Apparently, most of the passengers were going to New York. Lena had a fleeting urge to pick up her bag and get onto that train. She had no desire to go to Montreal, she just wanted to be traveling in the direction opposite from home.

More people were pushing through the station door. Among them, she spotted a tall man in a green slicker. Ben? His hair had gotten wet in the rain. He kept turning his head rapidly, looking for someone. He hadn't seen her, and she felt like hiding. But where, the bathroom? No, it was too late. Ben had seen her and was waving to her. She had to wave back.

He walked over with a small, awkward smile. He was out of breath.

"I was hoping I'd catch you here," he said.

Lena was so stunned that he had come here looking for her that she didn't know what to say.

"Are you alright?" he asked.

She nodded.

"Listen, I'm so sorry about last night. I acted like a coward. In fact, I acted like a piece of shit. It's just that my girlfriend is very sensitive, and Gerry—you saw what Gerry was like. Anyway, it's a long story." He looked sick with embarrassment.

"You don't have to apologize," Lena said. "It's okay. It really is fine." She just wanted for this conversation to be over.

A look of gratitude swept across his face, which just made her feel even more awkward.

"Are you still willing to give me your paper? I'd love to read it," he said.

"It's at the bottom of my bag."

He seemed to welcome her answer.

"Oh, I'll just give you my email then so you could send it to me." He handed her his business card.

"Thank you," she said, slipping his business card into her pocket, the same place where Inka's card now lay buried under a pile of loose change and some cough lozenges. She glanced at the big clock on the wall.

"Are you waiting for a New York train?"

"Yes. I'm taking the train to New York, and then another train to Boston from there."

"Boston?"

"Yes, I live there."

Lena moved her bag to her shoulder and shifted from one foot to another.

"Boston! I'll take you to Boston! I'm going to Maine. I go past Boston anyway. It's absolutely no problem for me to drop you off there. Do you want me to take you?"

He reached for her suitcase. His eagerness made Lena laugh, but she couldn't help being moved by it. She couldn't remember the last time the prospect of her company inspired such enthusiasm.

"Fine. Take me to Boston!" she said.

He laughed and picked up her suitcase.

"You pack light, don't you?" he asked, lifting her suitcase in the air.

His car was an old blue Chevy, the back seat crammed with boxes of books and random household objects. Ben had to remove a fur hat and something that looked like a portable stove from the passenger seat. Lena hit her foot on some huge chunk of metal lying under the seat. She bent to take a peek and was surprised to see something that looked like the Tin Man from *The Wizard of Oz*.

"That's an Italian juicer," Ben explained. "The one they use to make spremuta. It was a gift from my ex-wife. Just throw it in the back."

Lena could hardly lift it, let alone throw it, so she just moved it away from her feet.

They spent the first hour of their trip in uncomfortable silence.

"Are you okay?" Ben kept asking.

"Yes."

"You look all hunched up."

"No, I'm fine. It's just that I've been driving a minivan for years and this feels a little low."

"Put the juicer in the back, you'll have more leg space."

"It's fine."

"You're not hungry, are you? We can stop for a sandwich."

"No, no, I'm fine."

"I think I have some water in the back."

"I'm fine."

There really was no space for her feet. So she rested them on her backpack. She was thirsty and longed to look at herself in the mirror.

She cleared her throat and asked if Ben had some music.

"The CD player is broken. You can try the radio."

Lena tuned the radio to a jazz station, but then a commercial break came on and she turned the radio off.

"Where do you live in Boston?"

"Chestnut Hill."

"Nice area. I used to live in Boston. Cambridge, actually."

"Cambridge is nice too."

The conversation died.

It had been so easy to talk to him at the reception. And now whenever Lena felt that she was about to come up with something to say, it slipped away.

There weren't too many cars on the road, until suddenly there were. The traffic got really dense and slow around Albany.

Lena craned her neck to look at the traffic ahead.

"It stretches for miles," she said.

"I think there's an accident ahead," he said.

Why did he sound apologetic? It wasn't his fault.

"Why are you going to Maine?" she asked.

"I have a cabin there. My girlfriend hates it, so we never go there. She's decorating our apartment in New York now, and since we don't have any space for my old junk, and I can't bring myself to throw it away, I'm taking it there."

"You have a lot of books."

"These are mostly graphic novels. I have hundreds of them."

"We went to Maine on Labor Day weekend," Lena said. "It took us seven hours. The kids were going crazy."

"How old are your kids?"

"Six and eleven. Do you have kids?"

"Yes, a daughter from my first marriage. She's nineteen. What does your husband do?"

"He's a math professor. What does your girlfriend do?"

"She's a lawyer."

"Her name's Leslie, right?"

"Yes. Leslie. What's your husband's name?"

"Vadim."

The conversation died once more.

Lena wanted to ask about Gerry Baumann, but she was afraid it would make Ben apologize about last night again. Still, awkward conversation was better than no conversation at all, she decided after another ten minutes passed.

"Is Gerry Baumann an old friend of yours?" she asked.

Ben seemed grateful to have a new topic.

"Oh, yeah. We go way back. We were best friends in high school. We even drew a comic strip together."

"Didn't he win a Pulitzer?"

"Yep. For a graphic novel. But I always thought that the comic strip we did in high school was his best work."

"What was it about?"

"I guess it was about sexual education in a sense. We called it *Grammatology of a Pussy*."

Lena thought that she misheard the title and turned to Ben.

"Grammatology of a . . . ?"

"Yes, that's right. *Grammatology of a Pussy*."

"What does it mean?"

"Huh. Good question. It all started with Gerry's father's bookcase. It was our favorite after-school game. We went through his father's philosophy books and tried to incorporate the word 'pussy' into the titles. Grammatology of a pussy, for example. That one was our favorite."

Lena laughed. So now that they had some kind of a conversation going, the important thing was to not let it die.

"So what was it like? Did you have some brilliant insights on pussy?"

Ben shook his head. Lena noticed that his face looked different in profile. His nose seemed sharper, larger, his forehead more pronounced. The smile made the deep furrows that ran along the corners of his eyes more pronounced. Lena had a sudden impulse to touch his face. "I don't think there were any insights. Mostly pictures. And then we were afraid that our parents would find the manuscript, so we wrote in code. We just substituted 'Township of P' for the word 'pussy': 'When you enter the Township of P, you have to do this and that.' We had to draw in code too."

"How do you draw in code?"

"I would make hedgehogs out of pussies."

"Hedgehogs?" Lena asked. "How on earth can you make a hedgehog out of that?"

"It's really very simple. Imagine a hedgehog lying on its back. It looks remarkably like a pussy as it is. I just had to add tiny paws and draw a hedgehog's nose over the top."

"Have you ever seen a hedgehog? I thought they weren't native to America."

"It so happened that I did see a live hedgehog. Two of them actually. But that's another story."

There were crinkles in his eyes. He looked remarkably more attractive when animated.

"Tell me."

"Gerry had this crazy uncle who brought two hedgehogs from Germany as a present to his wife. His wife hated them. She said they looked like rats with spikes. They gave the hedgehogs to Gerry, but he wasn't sure how his parents would react, so he kept them in the basement. They had a neat basement. Gerry's grandfather (he'd died by that time) used to fish, and there was all kinds of fishing equipment around, nets, rods, tackle, huge dusty boots, even a boat motor, but there was no boat. God, I remember it so well—the small dusty basement, the fishing rods suspended on the walls, two hedgehogs in a cage, the smell of pot."

"Pot?"

"Well, yes. We started going to the basement, because it was a perfect place to smoke pot—Gerry's grandma had recently fallen on the basement steps and she was too afraid to venture down there again. She would bake a big batch of carrot muffins for us, and we would take them down to the basement. I'd sit on the floor with my notebook, and Gerry'd prance around in those boots, with a muffin in his hand and muffin crumbs all over his chest, spouting his brilliant thoughts on pussy."

Lena smiled.

What the hell were they talking about? Hedgehogs, pussies, pot. But she loved it. She couldn't remember the last time she'd had so much fun.

"Do you still have it?"

"Do I have what?"

"Grammatology of a Pussy?"

"The manuscript? No, I'm afraid not."

"A pity!"

"Oh, yeah. Huge loss for humanity."

"Do you know where I first saw the word 'pussy'?"

"Can't wait to find out."

"The Canterbury Tales."

"The Canterbury Tales?"

"Yes. At the camp, Inka and I used to read them aloud at night, hoping to find something about sex. We would read a passage and start laughing. One time Inka laughed so hard that she actually fell off the bed. And when she fell, I started to laugh, and laughed so hard that I couldn't stand up and help her, and she got very mad at me."

"The Canterbury Tales?" Ben asked. "Sex? Fun? Falling off beds? Are we talking about the same book? I read them in school and they were dreary. And how could you even get through Middle English?"

"Oh, we read them in modern Russian."

"The Canterbury Tales in Russian! That must have been what made them sexy."

"No, Russian made them confusing! I remember there was a line that I couldn't understand. In Russian it read, 'He grabbed her little box.' I didn't know what to make of it. Did he snatch her jewelry box and run? It was Inka who found the explanation in the footnotes. In the original it said, 'And prively he caughte hire by the queynte.'"

"Queynte? What's that? Wait! Is it . . . ?"

"Uh-huh. Very evocative, isn't it?"

"Queynte, huh?" Ben said.

The green road sign rushed at them and then past them: 25 MILES TO BOSTON.

"Boston," she said.

"Boston, right," he said. "How far do you live from here?"

"About twenty minutes."

"Only twenty minutes!"

He looked at her in mock disbelief. Lena picked her bag up off the floor and put it onto her lap, holding it tight by the handle and the strap. Parting with Ben in twenty minutes seemed inconceivable. Only thirty minutes to Boston.

"Listen. Do you have to be home at a particular time?" Ben asked, "because if you don't, we can go to Rockport, and take a walk along the beach, and maybe have a bite to eat afterwards."

"Rockport! Yes! I always wanted to go to Rockport, but for some reason we've never gone."

"Perfect," Ben said, and Lena put her bag down.

Five

B ut by the time they got to Rockport, it had started to rain so hard they could barely see the streets. It seemed as if the whole town were a watercolor painting, and everything—streets, houses, trees— was getting erased, washed off the paper.

"Where is the ocean?" Lena asked. "I thought we were getting to the coast."

"You'll see it in a second," Ben said, making a turn onto another street. And there it was. The ocean, or at least the little of it they could see through the solid wall of rain and fog. Huge gray waves broke through the rain, threw themselves up, and smashed against the jetty. She gasped, and chuckled, and shook her head.

"Well, yes. But I guess a walk along the beach is out of the question now. Are you hungry?"

"Hungry? I don't know."

"We left Saratoga four hours ago. You must be. There's a restaurant right on the dock."

The restaurant turned out to be on the second floor. The stairs were outside, under the roof, which didn't protect them from the rain that seemed to rush in from different directions. Ben took Lena's hand and led her up the darkened, slippery steps.

Inside, it was empty and warm. Dark exposed wood everywhere, and the tables made of the same kind of wood with red-and-white-checkered tablecloths and pink napkins sticking out of pink plastic glasses. Ben led her to a window table even though they couldn't see anything through the window except for cascades of water running down the glass on the other side.

The waitress had a blond crew cut and creased skin, like an old leather jacket. She handed them the menus and asked what they wanted to drink. Ben asked for a beer. Lena said, "Just water." The waitress snorted with disapproval.

Ben started to read the menu with deep concentration, as if it contained a math problem. There was still something boyish about his face. That shock of hair across his forehead and the way he scrunched his nose when reading.

She wanted him to kiss her. She imagined that his lips would be cold and taste like beer.

Lena took a long drink of her water and looked away.

"Fried clams are supposed to be very good," Ben said.

"Okay."

"Gerry orders them all the time."

"You used to come here with Gerry?"

"Yeah, when I lived here."

"How did you feel when Gerry won the Pulitzer?"

"How did I feel? I was insanely happy for him. That's how I was supposed to feel, right?" Ben paused for a while, his eyes searching her face. "No, I couldn't force myself to be happy for him. Gerry won a Pulitzer even as my book proposal was rejected and I was struggling to hold on to my shitty job teaching art at a local Catholic school. His win devastated me."

Ben took a long sip of his beer and continued.

"But it was nothing compared to his being the first to get laid. That was when I really felt crushed."

Lena laughed.

"I know what you mean. My friend Inka turned into this really big shot. She is one of the most famous Russian journalists."

"The very Inka who would fall off the bed while reading Chaucer?"

"Yes. Can you imagine that? And I'm insanely jealous of her career, but it's nothing compared to how jealous I felt when I thought that she was more popular than me in the camp. She would go on all those dates, and I would be stuck taking care of the kids."

"Who would you even date in a summer camp?"

"Ours was a very special camp. It belonged to the Ministry of Defense, so it was full of officers and soldiers. And all the counselors were the girls from the State Pedagogical University, a school famous for its lack of men. Everyone called it the School of Virgins. So you can imagine the chemistry."

The waitress appeared with their food: fried clams and soggy French fries served in checkered paper baskets, with coleslaw in tiny paper cups, and soft, seedy pickles.

Ben picked up a bunch of clams with his fork, put them into his mouth and started to chew.

He had four deep lines across his forehead. They moved slightly when he ate. There was a crease over his left cheek that looked like a scar. Lena hoped that he didn't notice how she stared at him. But then again, he appeared to be discreetly studying her too.

"So Inka was more popular than you in the camp?" Ben asked.

"Only at first. Then I finally went on a date, and bizarre things started to happen. I turned into a femme fatale."

Ben put his glass down and stared at her.

"What do you mean?"

"I would go on a date with a guy and the next day he would disappear."

"Disappear? How?"

"Um—it's a mystery."

"I love mysteries!"

"Well, it's a long story, we won't have time for that anyway."

Ben shrugged and took another sip.

"Have you kept in touch with Inka?" he asked.

"No. Not since I left Russia. I've been following her career, though.

It was hard not to. She's all over the news. You know what's funny, though? I ran into her two days ago. In New York. At Macy's in Herald Square."

Ben shook his head.

"Interesting coincidence. You saw Inka and I saw Gerry. I hope Inka wasn't as obnoxious as Gerry."

"She was a little bit obnoxious. But, you know what, she said that she just found out I had a secret admirer at the camp."

"Nice! Who was it?"

"She wouldn't tell me."

For dessert they had ice cream with homemade blueberry jam.

His lips were cold and tasted like blueberry jam when he finally kissed her in the long corridor by the door just as they were about to exit, and then again, by the car, where they kept kissing for a very long time.

Outside, it had stopped raining but became very dark. Still, they had a clearer picture of their surroundings, with glimpses of boutiques on the main street, and fishermen's boats, and the dark ocean speckled with tiny islands. They drove past the jetty, over onto the main street, past the grand inns and cute bed and breakfasts, all sporting proud NO VACANCY signs.

"There is a Holiday Inn a few miles north," Ben said, as if they'd already discussed this.

Lena fought a surge of anxiety and said, "Okay."

How strange, she thought, that when you meet a man you don't know whether it will happen or not. And then suddenly you know. And know with such certainty, it's as if it already happened.

It was very cold in the lobby of the Holiday Inn. Lena poured herself some acrid coffee from a big urn and sipped it as Ben signed them in. The key the receptionist gave them wasn't the usual plastic hotel key, but a real metallic one with something like a heavy wooden pear attached to the ring. The pear banged against the door when Ben turned the key to the right and then to the left. Lena was the first to enter the room. She walked to the middle and stopped between the bed and the bureau. There wasn't any other furniture except for a single chair by the window. She caught her reflection in the mirror beside the commode. She looked rumpled, helpless, and small. She felt like that too. She dropped her bag to the floor and turned to Ben.

One day that summer, Lena and Inka went to the underground spring to get some fresh water.

The path to the spring branched off the main road to the camp and wound through the fields and meadows and narrow strips of birch forest. They walked at a leisurely pace, swinging the empty teakettles, savoring all the little pleasures of the countryside: the view of rolling hills, tiny houses far on the horizon line, the warm sun on their shoulders, the prickly grass against their ankles, the crumbly soil under their feet, the yellow flowers, the clucking of chickens, the dust in the middle of the road, even the smell of manure from the fields.

"Why is it that the smell of cow shit has these romantic associations, and human shit is simply disgusting?" Inka mused.

"I don't know. Maybe you should write a poem about it," Lena said.

Inka laughed and swung her teakettle at Lena.

Just a few days before, they wouldn't have been able to imagine their stay in camp could be enjoyable. Then they discovered the secret that experienced counselors had known all along: their job wasn't that hard if you didn't try to do it all that well. So what if the kids didn't eat on time? So what if they soiled their clothes? So what if they didn't wash their faces or brush their teeth? Nobody died from that. And that terrible fear that a kid would get lost. So far nobody had, and it was unlikely that anybody ever would. The kids were terrified of the woods. They wouldn't have dared venture anywhere on their own. As far as they understood, there were only two things Yanina cared about: full attendance during assemblies and keeping the kids' hands above the blankets. Once Inka and Lena had devised ways to ensure that, they stopped worrying. Another thing that they discovered was that there were times when they could be completely free. There were movies twice a week, when they just dropped the kids at the club and could do whatever they wanted. They could even leave the camp. Sometimes they went to the country store and bought cakes of brown soap, bread, cookies, and fresh strawberries. They didn't really need any of it, but the idea of going somewhere with the purpose of buying something made them feel civilized and accomplished. Or sometimes they would walk to the cornfield, pick a few ears of unripe corn, slim and tender, silky, greenish-white, and eat it raw. Still, their favorite trip was to the spring.

They swerved off the path and entered a thicket of birches. The grass there was tall and damp, and even the air smelled fresh and green. After they filled their teakettles, they usually sat down in the shade to chat. Sometimes, they would even bring a book. Today it was volume six of *The Arabian Nights:*

"'And Nur ad-Din turned to her at once, and clasping her to his chest, sucked on her upper lip, having sucked on her lower lip first, after which he shot his tongue into her mouth.'"

Lena liked how Inka read. Not too fast, and in a calm, casual manner.

"Kind of hot, don't you think?" she asked.

Lena nodded.

Inka continued: "'Then he raised himself up to her and found her to be an undrilled pearl, an unbroken mare.'" Inka put the book down and sighed.

"So, are you?" she asked.

"Am I what?"

"An undrilled pearl, an unbroken mare?"

If Lena had seen the question coming, or if Inka had asked "Have you ever done it?" she would've probably said that she had done it, but the question came as a shock, and it was so funny that she started to laugh, and after she finished laughing she said that she was in fact an undrilled pearl. Having admitted this to Inka, she immediately felt better. At least she didn't have to lie anymore.

"I had a guy put his hand down there," Lena said.

"And?" Inka asked.

"It felt good, but I started getting wet, and I didn't want him to notice it, and moved his hand away. I regretted it afterwards."

Inka said that she had done it. A couple of times, with a boy from her hometown. She didn't like it. She said that once the penis was in, you felt nothing. She claimed that a woman could only experience pleasure from the stuff that came before, touching, kissing, petting. And that you got so crazy from all that touching and kissing that you all but begged the boy to put it in. "You see," she explained, "hormones work like that, they fool you into thinking that you want a penis inside of you. They have to fool you for the sake of reproduction. But once the penis is actually inside of you and starts to move in and out, you feel nothing, you just lie there and wait until it's over. Sometimes, you get so tired of waiting that you start to move too, or to tighten your muscles in there so that it will be over sooner. The funny thing is that when you start to do that, the boys think you're really enjoying it. But I don't know, maybe it's different when you're in love."

Six

Lena woke up at six with a terrible headache. At first she almost welcomed the headache, which somehow made her feel less guilty for what they'd done. But then the noises from the construction site right in front of the Holiday Inn started making her pain intolerable. An excavator kept advancing and retreating as if performing some court ritual. She brushed her teeth and dressed and tiptoed out of the room trying to make as little noise as possible. There was no coffee in the lobby. It was damp and bitterly cold outside, shreds of early morning fog hanging over the gray parking lot. Lena spotted a mall across the street that was bound to have a coffee shop. She decided that the fastest way to get to the mall would be through the opening in the barbed-wire fence behind the pool. She scratched her leg against a broken wire as she was climbing through. Tiny beads of blood broke through the skin in a long thin line.

The Joy of Java place was crowded; patrons with their coffee and opened papers occupied every table. At the next table, an elderly emaciated man in shorts was staring at Lena over his coffee with an expression of curious disapproval. He looked like Vadim's father. Lena wondered if it was possible to guess from the look on her face that she'd just spent the night having wild sex. Well, the sex hadn't been exactly wild. It had been earnest rather than wild—earnest and awkward.

She took another sip of coffee.

She was bad at one-night stands—she'd always known that. It took her forever to figure out what it was that she wanted and how exactly she wanted it, and it took her even longer to gather up the courage to say it out loud. And as for her own actions—they weren't too impressive either, because she was too afraid to try something that her partner might not like and too shy to ask him. She must've seemed silent and morose to him. She *had* been silent and morose.

Another reason—possibly the main reason—why she couldn't enjoy it was that Ben was a stranger. A complete stranger in every sense—from his smell, to his movements, to the sounds he made. She knew that a lot of people found the idea of strangeness exciting. She didn't. She found it frightening and somewhat disgusting.

She wondered if Ben really had come the second time. She couldn't tell. He'd roared with great enthusiasm, but his eyes had looked tired. She herself never faked, because she found it awfully embarrassing— for some reason it was easier for her to admit that she didn't come (although this was embarrassing too) than to fake an orgasm.

She was pretty sure that Ben had faked his orgasm that second time. Did men even fake orgasms? She had nobody to ask about that. It was strange, but Inka had been the only person with whom Lena was completely open about sex. It had taken Lena a long time to admit to Inka that she was a virgin, but since then, they had exchanged the most intimate information, growing closer and closer in the process.

"I just know that I'll meet somebody," Inka told Lena on the eve of the first dance. "Last night, I had a dream that I was naked with a guy, in the woods, at night."

Lena wished she could share something equally exciting, but she never remembered her dreams.

On the morning of the first dance, everybody in the camp was checking the weather. Inka and Lena studied the clouds, and discussed what their shape and color meant. They even sent a couple of kids to check on the dance floor, to see whether the boards appeared to be solid enough. Everything seemed fine, yet as evening approached Lena was overcome by panic. The girls who had been there before said that the first dance was crucial to your dating future. If nobody asked you, then your prospects were probably pretty bleak.

The floor didn't collapse, and the loudspeakers were working fine, and by eight the whole population of the camp was there. Dressed up and excited camp residents were walking up the steps to the dance floor from all sides. Little kids came in pairs, holding hands, preceded and followed by their counselors. Big kids came in groups of four or five. Soldiers came as one big crowd, making the boards creak under their feet. Staff members came by themselves, wearing clothes that nobody would have imagined them wearing, like Galina's silver top, or Yanina's very tight, very yellow dress, or Natasha's scarf with the pattern of horsemen.

Inka and Lena led their kids up the steps and took the space to the left by the fence, opposite the corner occupied by the soldiers. Lena scanned the crowd of soldiers, trying to determine who she liked. She picked two. One was a tall guy with dark curly hair. He looked smart and he observed everything with a sly smirk, and whatever he was saying made other soldiers double up laughing. The other guy that she liked wasn't talking to anybody. He stood a little apart from the others, leaning against the fence. His features were still and sharp, like those of a wood-carving, but his eyes were dark blue, very bright and alert. Dena, a very pretty counselor with sunshine-yellow hair, noticed Lena's stare and said: "That's Danya, he is our artist." Lena blushed and looked away. When she turned in the soldiers' direction again, she noticed that the tall guy was staring at her. Their eyes met. He smiled and winked at her. Did this mean that he was going to ask her to dance? Lena decided that she liked him better than the wooden-faced Danya, who wasn't looking at her at all.

And then *boom*—the first beats of music rippled through the air.

They felt the vibrations first—through the floor under their feet, through the rickety fence behind their backs—and the next instant the music came, so loud that they couldn't recognize the words or the tune.

Dena was the first to venture to the middle of the floor. She ran out, dragging two fourteen-year-old girls from her unit with her. Their movements were light and swift. A couple of soldiers stepped forward and joined Dena and the girls. Other counselors and older kids started to move closer to the middle. Lena caught the tall soldier staring at her again. She started to laugh and grabbed Inka's hand and dragged her to the middle of the floor. Suddenly, though, the song ended, and they had to freeze in the middle of the floor. They felt like idiots. When the next song started, it was very fast. Too fast. Lena didn't know how to dance to that, but eventually decided to try. She jumped, and rocked, and dunk, and bent down, and threw her hands up, and jumped again still higher. At one point she almost knocked over Sveta Kozlova, who tried to dance as close to the counselors as possible. But Lena didn't care. It was as if she were drunk.

Then the music stopped and Volodya, the DJ, paused meaningfully and sighed into his mike before announcing the slow dance. Every-body who had been dancing in the middle of the floor filtered back toward the fence, hoping to be asked for a slow dance. Dena was asked before she even made it to her place. Lena tried very hard not to look at the soldiers. She was staring down at her sandals, at her skirt, smooth-ing folds, shifting her weight from one foot to the other. She didn't say anything to Inka, but she felt Inka's presence next to her, her breath-ing—she was still catching her breath after all the jumps—and her heat. Lena saw a soldier walking across the floor toward her. She could only see his boots, but she knew, she simply knew that he was the tall soldier who'd been staring at her.

"My name is Andrey. Shall we dance?" he said. Lena raised her eyes. Andrey wasn't looking at Lena. He was looking at Inka. He was ask-ing Inka to dance with him. Inka and not Lena. Inka's face lit up with a smile as she followed Andrey to the middle of the floor. Lena felt foolish and angry. She suddenly remembered about Danya, the soldier with dark blue eyes, and turned to see if he was still standing alone. He wasn't there.

Lena spent the whole five minutes of the slow dance awkwardly leaning against the fence, mulling over her bleak dating prospects, because she did believe that camp superstition that claimed that the first dance decided your fate. After the slow dance it was time to take the kids to bed. Most of them were still in place hanging by the fence. But sweaty and red-faced Alesha Pevtcov kept running and dodging and hiding from the counselors. "Alesha!" Inka screamed. Andrey jumped over the fence and a moment later emerged with a squealing and wiggling Alesha squeezed under his arm. He put him down and gave Inka the military salute. It was the perfect fairy-tale moment. A brave knight conquering a three-headed fire-breathing dragon to save a fair-haired maiden. And when Alesha got hyper, he was hardly any easier to conquer than a dragon. So, yes, Inka beamed with gratitude. But she was too fat for a fairy-tale maiden! Inka then took Lena aside and asked her to take the children back. "I need to talk to Andrey, okay? You don't mind, do you? Really? Thank you! Thank you so much!"

Lena led the kids back to their unit. She could still hear the beat of the music, but the excitement had petered out. She felt tired and a little nauseous, and embarrassed about the way she'd danced.

After the kids were asleep, Lena went to her room and tried to read, then tried to sleep, then ate some candy. She felt like an elderly spinster aunt who always takes care of the children. She listened to the sounds coming from the kids' bedrooms, hoping that something bad would happen to distract her from thinking about Inka, or maybe that something really bad would happen and Inka would feel guilty for going on a date. Lena thought that she was just as pretty as Inka. Actually, she considered herself much prettier. Inka wasn't that pretty to begin with. Inka looked like a cow. She fell asleep while trying to imagine her roommate grazing in the meadow with a cowbell around her neck.

///////////////////////

Somebody in the café dropped a tray with coffee mugs, breaking Lena's reverie.

She looked into her own empty mug and wondered if she should've bought coffee for Ben as well. Her mother loved to say that every relationship was a journey from a cup of coffee served to you in bed to a coffee mug thrown in your face. Yet, wouldn't it be really selfish and impolite not to bring him coffee? She stood up and went to the end of the line.

When Lena walked into the room, Ben was fully dressed.

"I thought you'd disappeared," he said. "I guess that would've made me *un homme fatal.*" He glanced over at the bed and chuckled nervously. He looked as if he was just as insecure about last night as she was. She knew she should've reassured him, but she didn't know how. One more thing that made her a bad lover.

She handed him the cup of coffee and a paper bag with a muffin. He took them from her and was about to kiss her when she said "here" and pulled a few cream containers out of her pocket, and packets with three kinds of sugar: white, brown, and fake. He took the white, poured the contents into his cup, and drank the coffee quickly, standing up. It took them no more than five minutes to pack up their things, check out, and get to the car.

The fog had lifted, but windows were all misty on the inside. Lena picked up a rag from under her seat and wiped hers.

They swerved onto Main Street and drove toward the highway in silence. At the red light Lena reached into her bag, pulled out a tube of Neosporin, and put some over her cut, then put her feet on top of her bag.

Ben's face was creased. His eyes were puffy. He looked tired and distant. The ride to Boston would take them forty minutes or so. He would drop her off, and they'd say good-bye to each other. She would spend some time at home, trying to do some household chores, then she'd realize that she was too tired and sad to do that, and she'd take a bus to Cambridge and aimlessly wander the streets, thinking about Ben. Some of her memories would be embarrassing and she'd try to banish them; others would be stirring and she'd try to savor them, bringing them up again and again. She would evoke certain things about Ben and feel the immediate shock, the shiver. Physical memories—an amazing thing, if only they didn't fade so quickly. In a few weeks she would feel nothing. She would be just as sad and empty as before except that now she would be guilty and ashamed as well.

The sign read 95 NORTH PORTLAND AUGUSTA—RIGHT LANE. 95 SOUTH PORTSMOUTH BOSTON—LEFT LANE.

The prospect of going home filled Lena with unbearable dread.

She shifted in her seat and turned to Ben.

"Take me to Maine with you," she said.

"To Maine?"

"Yes. To your cabin. I don't have to be in Boston until Monday."

She didn't know why she said that. She couldn't really want to go to Maine with him, did she? Why would she?

She needed to show Ben that she'd been joking. How do you show that you're just joking? Her mind was blank.

"It's on the rustic side," Ben said.

"What?"

"My cabin."

Here was her chance to laugh and say that she hated everything rustic.

She said: "I love rustic."

Ben looked away and ran his finger around his lips. She was mortified. In a second he would look at her with a kind patronizing smile as if she were a child and say, "You know I can't," or worse yet, "You know we can't." And then they would have to spend the next thirty minutes to Boston in dreary silence.

But instead he looked at her and chuckled.

"Okay. Let's see if there are cops around."

"Why?"

"See, no U-turn here."

Lena could barely hold back a squeal of delight.

"No cops. Make a U-turn!" she cried.

The car made a sharp U and sped back to the crossing.

"Now we're officially outlaws," Ben said.

They went through the toll booth and onto 95 North. They were going to Maine.

Lena couldn't believe how relieved she felt, despite her uncertainty just minutes before. She stretched in her seat and bumped her leg against the juicer again. This time she picked it up and put it on the backseat.

SEVEN

They were about to pass the WELCOME TO MAINE sign when Ben's phone rang. He kept it on vibrate. She heard a barely audible buzz and saw how Ben paled and stiffened as if there was a nagging pain in his left thigh. He pulled his phone out of the pocket of his pants, looked at the number, and put it back.

His phone was elegant and thin.

Lena's phone, buried deep in her backpack, was sturdy and plump, metallic, no extra features, an older model. It rang a few minutes later. She always kept it at the top volume, and she jumped when it rang. She turned the music off and rushed to get the phone out of her bag, but she couldn't find it right away. She rummaged in her bag with her hands shaking, dropping her other things on her lap or to the floor, her lipstick, or her sunglasses, or her tiny French dictionary, while the phone rang and rang. When she finally took it out, there was a dollar bill and an old receipt caught in it. She paled and stiffened just like Ben a few minutes before. She didn't pick up.

A long and awkward stretch of silence followed.

"Why don't you tell me your mystery story?" Ben asked.

"My mystery story?"

"Yes, you said there was a long mystery story about those guys that disappeared after a date with you. It's about five hours from here to the cabin. We have all the time in the world."

"Okay, sure. There's time. It's a little confusing, though. I'm not even sure where to begin."

"How about the first guy who disappeared?"

"Yeah, you're right. Seems logical."

Lena stretched in her seat and wrinkled her nose in concentration.

"Kostik was the first," she said. "He disappeared on June twelfth. I remember the date because it was my grandfather's birthday.

"It happened after a double date with Inka and Andrey, which had been Inka's idea. She had just met this soldier, Andrey, at the first dance. He asked her on a date, and she asked him to bring a friend for me. I had never had a double date before and I didn't know that they were supposed to be awful by definition. One couple is always better, hotter, more at ease, happier than the other, which inevitably makes the other couple find a million things that are wrong with them and their relationship.

"In our case there was no doubt which couple was the happy one."

Lena stopped talking and cleared her throat. She couldn't believe she was actually telling the story out loud. Over the years she had spent so much time telling it in her head that now every word she used felt awkward and wrong. The main problem was not even the content: what to tell, which scenes to choose, which characters or events to bring forward, which to omit altogether, but how to transform images into words. Because in her head, the story ran like a movie. A movie that would randomly jump from one image to another, depending on how she felt or what was on her mind. Sometimes she would even see the same image over and over again, a little differently each time. And since she had been thinking about this story for years, she could no longer tell which of the images came from memory, which from her interpretation of the memory, and which purely from her imagination.

She closed her eyes and tried to evoke the exact image of how they'd sat at the picnic table.

"We sat at the picnic table outside our unit," she said. "The four of us. Inka and Andrey sat on one side, snuggled against one another, staring into each other's eyes, engaged in happy banter, laughing at each other's jokes or sometimes for no reason at all; and Kostik and I sat opposite them, about two feet apart, silent, dumbly smiling as Andrey and Inka joked. I didn't know why Inka wanted me there at all. By then, I began to doubt that I understood Inka at all. Ever since she had hooked up with Andrey (which was only three days before, I wanted to remind her), she'd behaved as if she had always been popular, as if the whole lifetime of her loneliness and insecurity had never happened. I noticed that she'd become drawn to Dena, the slutty, pretty, popular counselor. Suddenly, it seemed like Inka'd rather spend time with her than with me, and she even subconsciously mimicked Dena's words and expressions. Which didn't suit a fat pig like Inka at all, I would think, and then become surprised at the nastiness of my thoughts."

Ben chuckled, and Lena became momentarily embarrassed, but she continued the story anyway.

"Well, okay, Inka's reasons for inviting me on this date weren't clear, but my reasons for accepting were even foggier. Could it be that I thought that even this humiliation was better than staying in the room alone while Inka was on a date?

"Kostik had brought a bag with sunflower seeds, and Inka brought out a jar with sour cherry jam that she had confiscated from Sasha Simonov. They were all eating the jam, taking turns sticking their spoons right into the jar. I hated jam, so I concentrated on the seeds."

Lena paused and looked at Ben. He was looking at the road ahead, but his expression was pensive. Did he even know what sunflower seeds were? Lena wasn't sure if she was telling the story right. It still ran in her head like a movie, brighter and louder than ever, and now in first person, like a movie addressed to Ben. But the movie was happening in her head, her words were a pale voiceover, they couldn't possibly convey everything that was there to convey. She wondered how much he saw or understood.

"'Hey,' Inka said, 'you're shelling the seeds the wrong way!'

"I knew I was shelling them the wrong way. I could never shell them the right way. You're supposed to put a seed in your mouth and bite on it, and then it'll somehow get out of the shell and you'll spit the shell out. I couldn't do it the right way, because when I bit on the seed, the seed just turned to mush and didn't come out of the shell. So I shelled them one by one with my hands.

"'You look cute like that, Lena,' Andrey said. 'With a seed in your fingers, you look like a little squirrel.'

"'Yeah, you do look like a squirrel like that!' said Kostik.

"Furious, I wanted to grab a handful of seeds, throw them at Inka, and leave. But then Andrey took out his new watch, and everybody forgot about squirrels. It was a beautiful imported watch that showed the date and the year as well as the time. 'It's June twelfth today,' Andrey announced. June twelfth! It was my grandfather's birthday, and I hadn't called him yet.

"I stood up and said that I had to go to the phone booth. Kostik stood up too and said that he would go with me.

"It was a long walk from our unit to the booth, which stood on the edge of the woods by the headquarters. Away from Inka, and her happiness, I immediately felt better. Kostik put his arm around my shoulder. It was heavy and warm and felt good.

"There was this amazing sexual tension in the air. I thought I could actually smell couples. You would walk across the camp territory in the dark, and the smells would reach you before you heard the sounds. Sharp, distinct smells: sweat, lip gloss, perfume, hairspray. And sounds, barely audible, almost drowned out by cicadas and bullfrogs, but still perceptible—panting, whispering, giggles, moans, and gasps.

"I thought that Kostik must have noticed it too.

"He cleared his throat and asked if I lived in Moscow. I said yes. He asked if I'd lived there all my life. I said yes. He said that he was from a small town on the Volga and that big cities like Moscow frightened him. I said that the neighborhood where I lived was on the outskirts of Moscow and looked more like countryside than a city. I said that there were cherry and apple trees. He said that his hometown was overgrown with apple trees, and in the summer everything smelled like apples.

"I smiled, and shivered, and moved closer to Kostik. I thought he might kiss me, but he moved away looking strangely tortured.

"There was a long line at the phone booth. Camp personnel and counselors calling home to check on their families. The women stood shivering in the night cold, swatting at the mosquitoes, shifting from one foot to the other, usually too cranky to chat. They would roll their eyes whenever somebody was on the phone too long, and sometimes even tap on the glass. Natasha, the camp nurse, talked the longest. I was sure that she was on the phone with her lover. She was completely engrossed in her conversation, and her tone and expression would change from weepy to elated and back. And every time somebody impatiently tapped on the glass, Natasha, usually so meek and considerate, gave the tapper a fierce, almost threatening, glare. She may have looked like a rabbit with bad skin to Inka, but to her mysterious lover, she must have seemed beautiful. For some reason, watching Natasha talk on the phone filled me with an almost unbearable longing to be in love."

Lena stole another glance in Ben's direction. She wondered if Ben could understand that. But he just sat there silently, concentrating on the road.

"When it was finally my turn to talk on the phone, Kostik stepped away from the booth. I thought he was being polite, but then I noticed that he had a particularly tortured expression. I wanted to ask what was wrong with him, but other people in line yelled at me to hurry up, and I went into the booth.

"The call took me about ten minutes—my grandfather wouldn't be satisfied without giving me a detailed description of all the presents he got. 'That shirt can't be cheap, right?' 'Grandpa, I can't really talk now, there is a line of people.' 'Uh-huh, and what about that radio your mother gave me? Sixty rubles—no less!'

"By the time I hung up, my left ear was all red and throbbing. I thought the two women that had been in line behind me would be livid. But there wasn't anybody. The women must have left. Kostik wasn't there either. I looked behind the booth. I called his name, peering in the dark, listening for the sounds of his steps, then looked around and called his name again and again.

"I walked up to the headquarters and knocked. Yanina's aunt shuffled toward the door. I asked her if she'd seen a soldier walk in. She said no. I asked her if she was alone. She said that Major Vedeneev was still there, 'Working, as always,' she added with reverence in her voice. I thanked her and headed back. It was completely dark, except for the sharp yellow light that came from the lantern that stood on the headquarters porch. I saw my shadow—enormous, reaching as far as the tops of the tallest pines. I started to run and ran all the way to our unit.

"Instead of Inka and Andrey, I found a squirrel poking around in the bag of sunflower seeds. It stopped and looked at me with the meanest expression I'd ever seen on a squirrel. For one crazy second, I thought that this was Inka turned into a squirrel.

"But, no, when I walked into the room, Inka was there, lying on the bed, daydreaming. I was surprised that her date was over so soon. I told her about Kostik. She said: 'Ah. He dumped you because he must have gotten tired of waiting for you to finish your call.' Then she scratched her stomach and said: 'Andrey is amazing, you know! Amazing! And a real gentleman too. Listen, do we have any stomach meds? I think I ate something funny at dinner.' I took a pack of Festal and threw it at her."

Lena stopped, because her lips were parched from all the talking.

"Do we have any water?" she asked.

"I think there's a bottle stuck under your seat somewhere."

Lena kicked the bottle from under the seat with her foot, picked it up, and drank some.

"Am I boring you with the story?"

"No, not at all!" Ben said. She thought he sounded sincere.

"The names are a little confusing. I kept thinking that Kostik was Andrey, and Andrey was Kostik. But it's not your fault. I read a Japanese novel once, and I had to go back to the beginning every few pages or so, just to remind myself who was who."

Lena drank some more water. She hadn't thought about how foreign her story might seem to him.

"Andrey was Inka's date. Kostik was my date," she clarified.

"Uh-huh. So Andrey was the perfect gentleman, and Kostik was not, because he ditched you at the phone booth."

"He didn't ditch me. He disappeared!"

"What do you mean? What happened?" Ben asked.

"You see, I don't know what happened."

"You never found out?"

"No. Not really. See, at first I just assumed that Inka was right, that Kostik simply dumped me. I never saw Kostik on the camp grounds again, but that wasn't unusual; soldiers would go to do a particular job and never be seen again. I could have asked Andrey, but I didn't want to embarrass myself asking about the guy who had dumped me. Then I met another guy, Danya, who I really liked, and forgot all about Kostik. It was only after Vasyok disappeared under similar circumstances that I started to feel suspicious."

"Kostik, Danya, Vasyok! You're confusing me."

"Well, I told you the story is long and confusing. There are so many threads."

"I am eager to hear more," Ben said. Lena looked at him. He did look eager to listen, but she was too tired to continue.

"I need a little break," she said.

Eight

They had passed the exit signs to Ogunquit, York, and Wells. The road, and the houses and woods by the sides of the road, seemed wide and low, solid, squat, real. They were going away together. She still couldn't believe it.

The woods in Maine looked different from the ones they'd left behind in New York and Massachusetts, but Lena couldn't understand how. The trees were the same, yet there was something strange about them. The leaves were tender and new, barely there, and the crowns seemed to be dusted with red and yellow. They passed a few small farms, houses framed by wildly blooming lilacs.

"Lilacs!" Lena said.

"Lilacs?"

"Look, lilacs are still in bloom here and the leaves on the trees are only starting to come out. Lilacs stopped blooming in Boston about a week ago. It's like we've gone back in time. We cheated time!"

"But it's not like we added it to our lives," Ben said. "When we get back home, time will have passed."

"But right now, we're going against the time. Cheating it," Lena insisted. The idea made her giddy.

"My daughter Becky had a similar idea when she was ten. I took her to London. On the way back, the plane took off at ten P.M., flew for six hours, and landed in New York at ten P.M. on the same day. She couldn't talk of anything else for days. She decided that if you spent your whole life traveling westward at the same speed, time would stop for you, and you would never die."

"Inka had a theory about cheating time too. She came up with it while simultaneously reading *The Canterbury Tales* and *The Arabian Nights*. She said that the *Tales* were about telling stories with the purpose of suppressing time, killing it so the journey seemed faster. And the *Nights* were about telling stories to stretch time, to make it stop so that you don't die. It's over as soon as your last story is over, you see? But as long as the story continues, it's never over."

"You have to go through the motions in order not to die—great theory. Listen, how old were you when you first started thinking about death?"

"I don't know. Ten, twelve, I think. You?"

"Six."

"Six, really?"

"Yes, I think so."

"You knew you would die at six?"

"I didn't know for sure, but I was scared that I might. I've developed a lot of devices to fight it off."

Lena peered at Ben, trying to imagine what he looked like as a child. It had been easier to imagine him as a teenager, when he was talking about his school the night before. But a child, a six-year-old? She looked at his eyes. Eyes change very little with age. He must have had the same eyes. Dark, alert, inquisitive.

"What were your devices?"

"Yes. The most important thing is to be on top of it."

"To be on top of death?"

"Yes. You can't let it get ahead of you, take you by surprise, you have to anticipate every possible way you might die, and vividly imagine how it will happen. The idea is that nothing happens exactly the way you imagine it. So if you imagine everything and in every detail, nothing will happen."

"Yes, that makes sense."

"I was in a car crash once, the tires blew out, and the car went spinning right in the middle of the highway with busy traffic. For a few seconds, I was absolutely sure that I'd die. So in those seconds, I vividly imagined my funeral. See?"

"Wow. Impressive."

"And you thought you had a fear of death."

"Hey! You seem to be very possessive. Fine, I grant you the exclusive rights to fear of death. How did it start, by the way? Was it triggered by something? An event or a conversation?"

"No. I just got it. I was lying in bed one night and I got it. All of a sudden. First about my parents. Then right after that about myself. And there weren't any illusions either. Heaven? Reincarnation? Please! Those were for idiots. I knew that I'd turn into nothing. There was me, and then—snap—there would be nothing. Just like that."

"Nothing?"

"Yep. Nothing. I imagine nothing as this half-physical environment. Murky and sickening and scary as hell. And then I had to live with this knowledge. Days were okay, more or less, not really okay, of course, but there were ways to distract myself. But at night I would lie and think about it for hours."

Ben's eyes squinted a little. He seemed to enjoy telling about his miseries.

"For hours? And you were only six?"

"Yes."

"Couldn't you tell your parents?"

"You see, I knew that they'd have to lie to me. About heaven, or going into the ground and eventually turning into a flower, or about a magic drug or some such shit. And they would know that I didn't believe them, and I would know that they knew, and we would all feel like idiots. I had this recurring nightmare. I would be doing something and suddenly feel that She was somewhere near and getting closer."

"She?"

"She. Her. I called her She. Just She."

"What did She look like?"

"I have no idea. I've never seen Her. That was the whole point—to do whatever I could to avoid seeing Her. I knew that as soon as She appeared something horrible would happen. Unspeakably horrible. And the only way to save myself was to wake up before She made it to me."

"How can you possibly make yourself wake up?"

"I had different tricks."

"Tell me!"

"Oh, come on! You're just making fun of me!"

"No, I genuinely want to know how to fight death. What if I meet it one day?"

Ben laughed.

"One was to go and take a cold shower, there in my dream. Or sometimes I just had to shut my eyes really tight and make a serious effort to open them."

"In your dream?"

"Yes, in my dream."

"Did it work?"

"Sometimes I would open my eyes and wake up, there, in my bed, and that was good. But other times I would open my eyes and wake up someplace else. And that meant that I wasn't awake, that I was simply in some other dream. But the most frightening thing of all was when I opened my eyes and found myself in my bed, but knew that I hadn't woken up, that I was still in my dream. Then I knew that She'd come for sure."

A passing car honked at them. Lena looked at the speedometer. It showed 50 mph. Ben must have been too much into his story to keep up with the flow of traffic. She found it touching.

"There was this one time at the cabin," he said. "It happened at the cabin. I woke up in the middle of the night with an acute feeling that there was something in the room. Some presence. I thought it was a moose, but then I realized that the moose couldn't possibly have gotten in. So it must be Her. There was only one bed. My father and I shared a bed, and he took up a lot of space, so I wound up very close to the wall. The cabin was made from these exposed logs. They were dark and stringy. I imagined squeezing inside them, hiding from Her. I kept tossing and turning, until my forehead touched the wall. I never realized how fuzzy it was. Ticklish. For some reason, I found it comforting, I knew that as long as I had my forehead pressed against that wall, She wouldn't get me. I felt so relieved that I started to cry."

Ben fell silent and peered ahead. Then he shook his head. Lena thought she saw tears in his eyes, but she wasn't sure.

"I can't believe I just told all this stuff to you. You must think I'm crazy."

"I don't. I told you crazier stuff anyway."

"No, you didn't."

She wondered if he was possessive about craziness as well, and decided not to argue.

"So, you spent a lot of time in that cabin?" she asked.

"No, not really. Dad built the cabin when I was little and he would go there whenever he had a chance. To get away from my mother, I guess. She hated the woods, and so he picked this very remote place, deep in the wilderness, knowing she would never come. Sometimes— a couple of times a year—he would bring me along to toughen me up a little. In the summer he'd teach me how to swim, and kayak, and fish. In the winter he'd teach me to cross-country ski. He really hated the thought that I was becoming a sniveling little worm."

"Sniveling worm? Is that an expression?"

"My dad's invention. He was born in Romania. He came here in his twenties, so he spoke with a slight accent, but he loved making up words and expressions."

"My father used to do that too. He called our cat Mokrohvost (Wet-Tail in English), because it brushed against his feet with its wet tail once."

"Is he still alive?"

"My father? Yes. He lives in St. Petersburg with his new family. Yours?"

"Dad? No. No. Dad died thirty years ago. I was fifteen."

"Did you like going to the cabin with him?"

Ben scratched his face.

"I don't know. I loved it and I hated it. He never told me if he was taking me until the last moment.

"He would ask my mother to pack his things, and then add that she should pack my stuff too. I would get crazy with anticipation. And on the way there, I'd talk nonstop about all the things that we were going to do there, and how I would shoot a moose or catch the biggest fish. Dad was usually in a pretty good mood on the way there, so he would smile at me and pat me on the head and tell me stories about things he'd done when he was there alone and about all the animals that he'd seen."

Ben turned his neck back and forth. Then he continued.

"Winter trips were my favorite. It was more of an adventure, because the car would often get stuck and we'd have to shovel the snow, and I thought I was pretty good at it. And also I always loved the first hour of our skiing trips. The scent of pines, and snow, and ski varnish. The ease of the skis against the fresh snow, the swishy sound the poles made, and how we'd stop for tea. We'd stand leaning against a tree and Dad would pour us some from the thermos. I loved that thermos. It came in a ragged leather case and had a white plastic knob screwed on so tight that only Dad could open it, and a real cork under the knob and a blue strap so that you could carry it. We would drink the tea and Dad would tell me stories how he used to go skiing back in Romania and here, in Maine, the snow was almost as good. You must understand. Do you ever feel like that?"

"Like what?"

"That things here are almost as good?"

"Oh, yeah. All the time. The good woods are especially hard to find. And snow. How I love snow."

"Dad loved snow too. I guess he loved snow more than I did. There were things that I positively hated about snow. It would stick to my skis on the way back, and make them heavier and heavier with each step, how I was cold and hot and sweaty at the same time. And how Dad's back would get smaller and smaller ahead of me, farther and farther away, and how he'd turn and yell 'What a sissy!' By the time we drove back to New Jersey, Dad would act like he was sick of me, he wouldn't speak, except to yell at me not to touch the water because he wasn't going to do a bathroom break every five seconds. I used to think that this was all my fault, because I'd been such a disappointment. But now I think he was that way because he loathed the idea of going back home."

"Is your mother still alive?"

"Yes. She lives in Florida. She seems to be happy there. Does your mom live here or in Russia?"

"She died a few years ago."

"Do you miss her?"

"I do. A lot. Do you miss your dad?"

"I do."

Lena thought how strange it was that when she'd first seen this man two days ago, he had been just a half-naked stranger. All she knew about him was that he could swim and had blue swimming trunks with a rather large whale on them. Now he was swiftly and irrevocably accumulating peculiarities, stories, details of the past. Only within this past day Ben acquired a car filled with all sorts of baggage such as an old juicer and his high school notebook, a thorny relationship with his dad, a powerful fear of death, and a crimped muscle in his neck. He was shedding his strangeness whether she wanted him to or not. As was she. The thought was both scary and exhilarating.

Ben touched her hand, then moved his hand away and put it back onto the wheel.

"Will you continue with your story?" he asked.

She smiled and reached for the water bottle.

"So Kostik was the first guy that disappeared. Who is next?"

"Danya. Danya is the next guy I met, but he wasn't the next guy that disappeared. I met him at the clubhouse.

"Yanina caught me one day after lunch and said, 'Lena, you're neat enough, follow me.' She led me to the clubhouse, where she showed me a few pairs of shoulder straps made of paper. 'The kids will be singing the Pilots' Song at the concert, so we need pilot uniforms for them,' Yanina explained. 'Their own white shirts and dark pants will do; all we need is shoulder straps. Sixty of them. But make sure to make them neat. The last girl wasn't very good, as you can see.'

"The task seemed simple enough. I studied the straps on the table. A blue rectangle. Two golden stripes in the middle. Three golden stars forming a triangle.

"Cutting out rectangles was boring but easy. Making one hundred and twenty narrow stripes was manageable too. It was hard to keep them parallel, but I persuaded myself that Yanina wouldn't care if they were parallel or not. The stars were the real problem. After long and painful practice, I did learn how to draw a star that was almost perfect. But no matter what I did, I could not cut it out. All my stars came out misshapen and missing points. It got even worse when I tried to glue them on. They would stick to anything—the table, the floor, my fingertips, my hair, my T-shirt, my knees—but the straps. And so I sat with scissors in my hands, smeared with glue, covered with tiny golden stars.

"There were only two rooms in our clubhouse. A bigger one with a stage and a wobbly piano, and a smaller one with all the art supplies, paints, chisels, big slabs of gray modeling clay, and even a workbench table. There was a strong smell of paint, glue, and freshly sawed wood. A ray of sunlight went from the window straight to my table, as if to mock me. It was nap time. So the kids were napping or at least caged and quiet, and Inka could do whatever she wanted. I imagined her outside, on the blanket, with a book, or with my *Art of Cinema,* trying to read, pushing the book aside, turning onto her stomach, dozing off. And I was stuck here in the back room of the clubhouse, with scissors in my hands, with all these sheaves of blue and golden paper spread in front of me.

" 'Hi,' somebody said. A guy in a soldier's uniform stood in the doorway with a paintbrush in his hand. I was so engrossed in my misery that I hadn't heard him walk in. His eyes were dark blue. I recognized him right away. He was the wooden-faced guy I saw at the disco.

"I said 'Hi' back."

Danya. Lena was talking about Danya now. Danya of twenty years ago. She felt a painful constriction in her throat. She mentally begged Ben not to interrupt her, and he didn't. He just sat there silently. Staring ahead.

She continued: "He went to the storage room and returned with a half-finished painting on a large canvas, and a box with oil paints.

" 'What are these?' he asked, pointing at the straps.

" 'Just this thing I'm making for the concert.'

"I didn't want him to see all the ugly stars or the ruined glue-smeared rectangles. I grabbed an old newspaper and put it on top of the pile, but a few straps fell to the floor. Danya picked one up. It had one stripe in the middle and two stars of slightly different sizes and shapes.

" 'Is that a shoulder strap?' he asked. 'Which rank?'

" 'I don't know,' I said, taking the strap from him.

"I wanted him to stop staring at my hideous straps, and so I asked about the painting he was working on.

" 'The letter *D*,' he said and headed to a worktable opposite mine. 'I am supposed to write "Dobro Pozhalovat" to welcome the visitors, and Avadeniy said that the letter *D* should represent camp life. I don't know why. Vedenej's idea.'

"We continued to work in silence.

" 'Come look, if you want,' he said after a while.

"I walked over.

"The letter *D* was about three by two feet.

"I peered closer and saw that the *D* was drawn as two pines forming a triangle with their tops touching. On the bottom of the *D* was grass with berries and mushrooms. A bunny was peeking out from behind one of the tree trunks, and a squirrel was climbing up the other.

" 'Wild strawberries don't grow under pines,' I said.

" 'Is that right?' he said, and added some more strokes of red paint to the grass to draw more strawberries. I couldn't think of another thing to say.

" 'Do you want to try?' he asked, and handed me a clean brush. The brush was larger, lighter than I'd expected, with really soft bristles. I leaned over the painting, careful not to touch any part of him.

" 'I have never painted anything with a large paintbrush,' I said.

" 'It's easy.'

" 'I like the smell of paint. Is this oil?'

" 'Yes. Don't be scared. Dip the brush into this jar and make a stroke right here.'

" 'Here?'

" 'Yes. I need to color in the trunks.'

" 'You're making them blue?'

" 'Brown. Blue is for the shadows. They would look flat if not for the blue.'

" 'I can't. I'll ruin it.'

" 'No you won't. Dip the brush. Yes, like that.'

" 'Like that?'

" 'Uh-huh. Not too much paint. It shouldn't drip.'

" 'That much?'

" 'Even less than that.'

" 'So I just make a stroke here?'

" 'Yeah.'

" 'Like that?'

" 'Yeah. Just do it. Don't leave the brush hanging there!'

"But I couldn't bring myself to make that stroke, and I left the brush hanging there and it dripped. A big fat smudge of blue in the middle of the grass. I looked at Danya in horror.

" 'Don't worry,' he said. 'I'll make a hedgehog out of it. This is just what my letter D was missing—a blue hedgehog.'

" 'I like hedgehogs,' I said.

" 'Are you going to the dance on Friday?' Danya asked.

"I nodded.

"'I'll see you there,' he said.

"I nodded again. It was then that he smiled for the first time.

"Nap time was over. I picked up the straps and ran to our unit.

There I laid them on the table in the lobby and went upstairs. My heart was beating like crazy. I could still feel the weight of the brush in my hand, my shock when the paint dripped onto the painting, the smell of paint.

"The straps were the first thing that I saw when I went downstairs the next morning. All sixty of them were laid out in neat rows. All done perfectly. Golden stars shining brightly against the blue. It could only be Danya. He saw how upset I was over the stars. He wanted to help me. He was my knight in shining armor. He must have sneaked into the building after everybody was asleep. He must have worked for hours. I couldn't believe Danya did that for me! He must have really, really liked me. I kept stroking them with my fingers with a big silly smile on my face."

Lena stopped and looked at Ben. She'd been so engrossed in her story that she had momentarily forgotten about her audience.

"You know what," he said. "It might sound idiotic, but you made me jealous."

Lena touched his arm and smiled. And just then his phone started to ring. The vibration was so strong that Lena could almost feel it on her body. She could also feel how Ben stiffened. She moved away from him and straightened up in her seat.

NINE

Ben made his call from a visitor center a few miles away from Augusta. Lena went to the restroom, and when she came out—wiping her hands on her raincoat, because hand dryers never managed to do their job—Ben was still talking. He was half-hidden behind a column. He kept his hand raised at chest level and he moved it up and down, as if reasoning or listing points. Sometimes he would shake it as if disagreeing, and sometimes he would squeeze it into a fist.

He was lying. Another detail added to her rapidly growing version of him. Lena didn't hear him lie, but she saw him lie. "I missed you, baby. Of course, I miss you. Of course, I love you. Of course."

That was what he must be saying to Leslie. Right now, right this minute. When Lena was on the phone with Vadim, she said these things too. But when she said these things, it was as if she switched to some kind of automatic mode. The words poured out with ease, familiar affectionate words that didn't seem to require her presence. It was as if the words had been prerecorded.

She started to walk away, along the edge of the woods, separated from her by the chain-link fence. The sign on the fence said KEEP THE WILDLIFE WILD! Her first thought was that they meant keeping wildlife agitated, that it was somehow important to keep the animals angry, because otherwise they would grow too lifeless and depressed. It reminded her of when her mother said, "You know what? I'm not even angry at your dad anymore," and how scared her words made Lena. She died a few months after that.

Lena dialed her kids' number. Misha answered. "Mom?" Then she heard both her children fighting over the phone. She told them about the wild wildlife sign. Misha laughed. He said: "No, Mom! It means 'Do not feed the wildlife.'" Borya laughed too. They didn't ask where she saw the sign. Then she felt the urge to tell them about the hedgehog farm in Gerry Baumann's basement, and she did: "This fat man, Gerry Baumann, a famous artist, used to have a hedgehog farm in his basement." Borya was especially impressed. "You know what, Mom," he said, "I think those male hedgehogs could breed after all, if they both turned gay, for example." Lena laughed and shook her head. "No, I don't think that would have worked," she said. She asked the boys to call their dad to the phone. She heard Misha yelling, and then some voices in the background, Borya yelling, then puffing into the phone, after which Misha said that Dad would call her back.

There was no way to get into the woods. Lena kept peeking over, hoping to see some of those angry animals. She wondered what kind of wildlife there was. Moose? Bears? Hedgehogs? No, no hedgehogs, they were not native to these parts, she reminded herself. And even in Russia, she had only seen a hedgehog once, a few days after meeting Danya. She had thought this was some kind of a happy sign, an omen. It happened when she and Inka took the campers on a scheduled walk in the woods called an "exploring expedition." She remembered that hike as if it happened yesterday.

The idea was to "get to the end of the woods." They carried biscuits, cold drinking water in aluminum teakettles, and a couple of blankets to sit on. Alesha Pevtcov also carried a large jar, because he hoped to catch a frog.

After some time, they could feel that the woods were about to end. They glimpsed uncertain patches of light ahead, and the usual forest sounds changed, they seemed louder and more intense, and there were barely noticeable wafts of wind, and this strange anticipation of something impossible, something unreal, something magical. The kids got very quiet and slowed their pace. Usually, they would be trying to run ahead, and push each other and fight for the first place in line. But not now. Nobody wanted to be the first to get to the end of the woods.

Except for Lena. She wanted to reach that magical place because she thought it would match the state of mind she had entered after that evening with Danya. She was there with Inka and the kids, but she wasn't really there. She didn't know where she was. Nowhere and everywhere. She could feel herself diffusing into molecules and permeating everything they passed. She had never felt like that before. She was in love.

"What's wrong with you?" Inka kept asking her, but Lena couldn't answer. For as much as she longed to tell her about Danya, she couldn't possibly share it.

She remembered how she took one of the kids' hands and said: "We're almost there. Let's run!" And they ran until the last trees on the path opened onto a field. She yelled: "Aaa!"

And soon all the kids were running around and yelling.

"Idiots," Inka said, stretching on the grass with an issue of *Art of Cinema*.

Lena stretched next to her, facing the sky. Now she knew exactly how the girl from the Song of Songs felt.

As an apple tree among the trees of the forest,
so is my beloved among the young men.
With great delight I sat in his shadow,
and his fruit was sweet to my taste . . .
Kiss me, make me drunk with your kisses!
Your sweet loving is better than wine.

Then she closed her eyes and imagined how it would happen with Danya. This was the simplest and purest fantasy she would ever have. She imagined herself lying on her back—very straight—with her legs open. Danya lay down on top of her. They reached the point of contact. And they both exploded. That was it. She wanted it so much, but at the same time she was so absolutely sure that she'd get it eventually, that it would happen, and that it would happen exactly like that, that she felt perfectly content.

The sound of a commotion in the bushes brought her back. The kids crowded by the blackberry bush, fighting each other to take a look at something.

"Hey! What are you doing there?" Inka yelled.

"A hedgehog, a hedgehog! We found a hedgehog!" the kids yelled back.

"Bring it here!"

Inka and Lena sat up to have a look. One of the kids, probably Sveta Kozlova, was holding it in the palms of her outstretched hands. Other kids followed her as if in a holy procession. Lena had never seen a hedgehog before. She was sure that seeing it now was somehow connected with Danya.

The hedgehog was curled up and trembling. It didn't look like an animal at all, but rather like some alien creature—a spiky vibrating ball.

"I want to draw it," Sasha Simonov said.

"No. Put it down," Lena said.

"No! He'll run away."

"So he will. We can't take him with us anyway. He'll die of boredom and gloom."

Inka looked at Lena as if she had gone crazy. She could have been right. But Sveta Kozlova took her words very seriously.

"Can you really die of that?"

"Hedgehogs can—they are less tolerant of depression than humans," Sasha Simonov said. Sveta looked at Sasha with interest and put the hedgehog down. Apparently, she believed in such dangers. She was just a little girl, Lena thought. And Sasha was just a little boy. And Alesha. They were little kids, funny, helpless, naïve. For the first time since Lena started working at the camp, she felt something like affection for them.

First few seconds, the hedgehog didn't move at all. But slowly, so very slowly, he began to unfurl. There was his little nose. Black, leathery, and wet. There were his tiny paws. They looked exactly like the paws of a rat or a mouse. Then they saw the tiny beads of his eyes. And then his tongue. Lena didn't expect him to have a tongue! A tiny pink tongue, which he stuck out like a cat lapping up milk. And a second later the hedgehog was gone. It rustled through the grass and into the bushes.

Lena couldn't wait until the second dance. She kept changing her shirt, unable to choose between the white and the blue, and applying and reapplying her lip gloss. She tried to imagine how Danya would look at her when he saw her at the dance. How he would smile at her, walk over, and put his hand on the small of her back. All without saying a word.

But as they were about to leave for the dance, Sveta Kozlova announced that she wasn't going, and that was that. She refused to explain why. She insisted that she was staying and there was nothing Lena could do about it. Lena could've asked Inka to stay with Sveta, but Inka had already left.

"Sveta," she pleaded, "Sveta, please."

She said, "No way!"

"But why?"

"Because the music sucks."

"Sveta, you're not serious," Lena said.

Sveta said, "Yes, I am."

"Sveta, do you realize that I have to stay here with you if you stay?"

Sveta nodded with great enthusiasm. She was hopeless.

Lena just sat down on the steps. She sat like that in silence for a couple of minutes, and then something occurred to her. She said: "Sveta, do you remember that hedgehog we saw in the woods?"

Sveta nodded again.

"Sveta, I will die of boredom and gloom if you don't let me go."

Sveta stared at Lena, contemplating her words, and eventually she sighed and said that she'd go.

Lena squeezed her hand. "Thank you."

Lena saw Danya as soon as Sveta and she got up the steps to the dance floor. He was standing with other soldiers by the fence. He wasn't looking in her direction, but he did appear to be searching for somebody. Lena thought she'd just walk up to him and say hello. But the next thing she saw was Dena crossing the floor. Dena stopped in front of Danya and made a bow. Her head plunged forward so that her bright yellow hair flew up and down. She took Danya's hand. He stepped forward and smiled.

"This song is okay," Sveta said. Lena realized that she was still holding her hand. Still staring at Danya leading Dena around the floor.

She couldn't believe how much that hurt.

When Lena was about ten, she asked her mother: "How will I know when I fall in love? What are the definitive signs?" She said, "Don't worry, you'll know." She had just come home from work, and she was sitting on the sofa flexing her toes, making them crack, which she always did when she was tired. She looked at Lena, and her expression was glazed with exhaustion and not friendly at all. But Lena really wanted to get the answer.

"But what if I miss it?" she asked. "What if I confuse it with something else?"

"You won't miss it," she said.

"Why? Why are you so sure?"

"Why am I so sure? Okay. I'll tell you why. Do you think you could 'miss it' if you had been beaten, kicked, and punched?"

Lena shook her head.

"Well, then," she said, "you won't miss love either."

Lena was so stunned by Danya's betrayal that she didn't notice Vasyok until Sveta said: "Hey, the kitchen guy is waving at you."

"Do you want to dance?" Vasyok asked. His hands felt awkward and fat on my back. Lena glanced in Danya's direction, but she couldn't see him, because there was another couple blocking her view. Lena braced herself for Vasyok's usual happy banter, but he didn't say anything throughout the whole dance. She felt strangely, unfairly angry with

Vasyok. It didn't make sense until years later, after she'd felt like that again, when she realized she'd been angry at Vasyok simply because he wasn't Danya and he couldn't do anything, anything at all, to make her feel about him the way she felt about Danya.

Lena's phone rang. A California number. She gathered her strength and answered.

Vadim didn't question her, but Lena told him a complicated lie about her whereabouts. She hung up and continued to walk along the fence, feeling how her lie started to spread inside her like a disease. A sickening, perfectly physical sensation, which was only going to get worse. There was no end to this fence. It went on and on. She turned back and walked toward the visitor center.

Ten

When they got to the car, Ben's phone rang again.

He didn't check the number. He started the car and slowly pulled out of the parking lot.

Lena decided Leslie must suspect something, or she wouldn't be calling every ten minutes. She felt a pang of guilt.

Interstate 95 turned into a narrow two-lane road surrounded by woods on both sides. More and more cars had Maine license plates. More and more had canoes and kayaks fixed to the roofs, bicycles on the racks, their wheels spinning with pointless zeal.

"Have you been together for a long time?" she asked.

"Leslie and I?"

"Yes."

"Well, we met in college. She used to date Gerry. So we spent a lot of time together. Then she and Gerry broke up and we kind of lost touch."

He looked tired. It was as if there were a little generator that had kept him going, and now the generator was off.

"We met again six years ago. At a party. I had just gotten divorced, but Leslie was married. We started an affair, but since Leslie lived in New York, and I was in Boston, we had to go back and forth a lot. So

Leslie decided to leave her husband, and she insisted that I move in with her. So now we're together. In New York."

"Are you happy with her?"

"Happy? I don't know. I don't really know how to define 'happy,' and anyway you can't be happy for long. Happiness is a very acute state, it's like a fever, you can't take it if it goes on for too long. But it's working, it's definitely working with Leslie."

Lena very nearly said, "Is it, really?"

Ben kept going. "We've known each other for a hundred years, we have history together, we have common interests, we have common friends. And then again, how do you define 'happy'? How do you even answer that question? Can you answer that question? Are you happy with your husband?"

"Yes, I can. I'm not."

Lena turned away and stared out of her window. What was so difficult about admitting that you weren't happy? Why did people think they needed to come up with all these complicated explanations, excuses, justifications? Or perhaps they just didn't want to admit it to themselves? Lena knew she wasn't happy. She had known it for a long time. There was a time when she blamed herself for being unhappy. She saw it as some kind of character flaw. She didn't believe happiness was an acute state, as Ben said. She never confused it with the euphoria of being in love. For her happiness was more like peace, contentedness, feeling that you were in the right place. She'd never had that with Vadim. Even when they first got married, she couldn't shake off the feeling that they weren't right for each other. She did feel affection for him, and she was moved by the very fact that he was so familiar, that they'd known each other so many years. She would pass him as he sat at his desk and inhale his smell—she always imagined that he smelled like freshly sawed wood—and her eyes would fill with tears, because this was the most familiar smell in the world for her. She never felt peaceful or contented around him, though. She kept telling herself that happiness was a luxury. She felt Ben's hand on her shoulder, but she couldn't turn. Her eyes were filling with tears, and she was terrified that he'd notice.

"Why don't you go back to your story?" Ben asked. "Who was the second guy who disappeared? Danya?"

Lena sighed. Her story had obviously acquired this new function of saving them from awkward silences.

She drank some water and made an effort to collect her thoughts.

"The second guy was Vasyok."

"Who is Vasyok? Weren't you supposed to have a date with Danya?"

"The date with Danya didn't work out. And Vasyok was a soldier who worked in the kitchen. A very nice guy. He disappeared after he seduced me with Hungarian salami."

"Was he Hungarian? Is that as dirty as it sounds?" Ben offered a self-deprecating laugh.

"No! Hungarian salami was considered a great delicacy and was very hard to get. The Ministry of Defense was powerful enough to provide the camp with it, only the kids never got to enjoy it. The camp management ordered some salami for the kids along with red caviar and bananas and other delicacies, but when all those treasures made it to the camp, the staff just divided the food among themselves according to their ranks. Vedenej, the camp director, got the most, of course. Then came Yanina, and after Yanina, the camp plumber, the kitchen staff, some of the senior counselors. The soldiers weren't supposed to get any salami, but Vasyok worked in the kitchen, so I think he simply stole some."

"Stole? Some nice boyfriend you had! Salami thief," Ben said.

He seemed to enjoy hearing about Vasyok much more than about Danya. And for Lena, talking about Vasyok came more easily too.

"You don't understand. Stealing was considered perfectly fine. Everybody stole. It would have seemed strange and even indecent if you didn't. But of course everybody stole on their own level. Vedenej and Yanina could steal something really big, like camp funds. Senior counselors stole electronic equipment. Junior counselors mostly stole bedsheets, office supplies, and toys."

"Didn't they count bedsheets?"

"They did. They counted everything, even soccer balls, but there was a way to get past that. You see, each unit was given a certain quantity of items, and we counselors had to sign for them. If an item was reported lost and/or missing, they would deduct its cost from our salary. At first, I took it very seriously—after the kids in my unit came back from a walk outside, I made sure to search the grounds for all the forgotten toys so that I didn't have to pay for them. One time, I couldn't find a soccer ball. I looked for it and looked for it, but I couldn't find it. One of the older counselors, Galina, was passing by, and she asked me what I was doing. I said that I needed to find a soccer ball because I didn't want to pay for it. She laughed and told me to follow her into a storage room. There she picked up a soccer ball from the shelf, took large scissors from the drawer, sliced the ball open and cut it in two. 'See, now you have two soccer balls,' she said, as I stood flabbergasted. 'Go show the pieces to the inventory girl, and she will write them off as two "damaged" soccer balls. Nobody ever checks if the pieces come from a single ball or two different ones.' I stared at the pieces in awe. We didn't have to pay for damaged items, only for missing ones."

"That's brilliant! Did you steal something yourself?"

"Yes, sure. As soon as I discovered the art of damaging, I stole plenty of things. Felt pens, paints, big sheets of white paper, and a couple of pillow cases—scissors worked especially well on pillow cases. I wanted to steal an iron. I found the handle from some other iron in the garbage so I could report our iron as damaged, but Inka managed to steal it before me. Technically the iron was mine to steal, because I signed for it, but apparently Inka didn't feel the same way."

"That was rotten of her to steal your iron."

Lena smiled at Ben and said, "Thank you. I thought so too.

"So back to Vasyok. We danced together at the dance, and afterwards he asked me out. I agreed, because I was upset about Danya, and because I didn't know how to say no, but I didn't really want to go on a date with Vasyok. He was supposed to pick me up at nine-thirty the evening after the dance. In the morning, I told Inka that I didn't want to go.

" 'I don't know,' she said. 'He seems kind of stupid.'

"All morning I couldn't decide if I should refuse Vasyok or not, and then we had a power outage. It happened around lunchtime, and they couldn't prepare lunch, because everything in the kitchen and the cafeteria was down. After a while they sent some guys from the kitchen to distribute dry biscuits and buttermilk to the kids. Vasyok came to my unit with a box full of biscuits and a crate with buttermilk containers. He unloaded that in the lounge and then asked if he could talk to me in private for a second. There was some commotion—kids didn't want biscuits or something—but I left Inka to handle it. We stepped outside and he led me to the bushes. There, he looked around and started unbuttoning his shirt. I was about to yell 'What're you doing!' but he took out a long newspaper-wrapped package tucked under his belt. 'This is for you,' he said. The package had a faint smell of garlic, and something else, something smoky—my stomach rumbled.

"Vasyok asked me if we were seeing each other at nine-thirty. I said yes, because it would've felt too awkward to say no."

Ben started to laugh.

"I can't believe you sold yourself for a salami."

"It wasn't because of salami! The guy was nice to me, he took a big risk in stealing that salami for me. I didn't want to hurt his feelings."

"Right! The next thing you'd say would be that you didn't even enjoy that salami."

"Oh, I enjoyed it!

"When I got inside, Inka had just finished pouring the buttermilk for the kids. I motioned to her to come with me upstairs. I could hardly wait to unwrap the package. There were four slices of rye bread, two small cucumbers, a bunch of chives, and a large chunk of salami. Inka actually squealed with delight."

"What a good friend you were," Ben said.

"Why?"

"You shared your salami even after she stole your iron!"

"Huh, I guess so!" Lena laughed. "We locked the door so the kids wouldn't see our feast, and rushed to get at the food.

" 'Look, look!' Inka screamed, pointing to the tiny envelope made out of foil. 'He wrapped some salt for the cucumbers. I can't believe this guy, he is so thoughtful.' The only problem was that we didn't have a knife. We tried to slice the salami with Inka's tiny scissors, and then with Inka's nail file, but we didn't get very far. We had to take turns biting into the whole piece, while munching on the bread, cucumbers, and chives.

"Inka said that I should definitely date Vasyok. Our illicit lunch put her in such a good mood that she even offered her lip gloss and rosewater perfume for the date.

"As I put my lip gloss on, I thought what an idiot I'd been to think that Danya was in love with me. So what if he made those straps for me? He helped me with my work. Maybe he did that for everybody. It didn't mean anything. But then I remembered his face, his blue eyes, his carved features, the gentle way he held that brush for me. I still loved him, even if he didn't love me back. But now I was going on a date with Vasyok.

"I went onto the porch at exactly nine-thirty, wearing my flimsy white top and smelling like Inka's roses. Vasyok wasn't there. I didn't worry, I thought he just got held up. I had thought that the rose perfume was very elegant, but the longer I stood on the porch waiting for Vasyok, the less I liked the smell. By nine forty-five the smell started to make me sick, like the disgusting air freshener that my mother liked to use. Around ten, I decided I couldn't stand it anymore. Plus, it was getting cold. I ran up to my room to change. But as I was rummaging through my suitcase to find a sweater, I suddenly had the distinct feeling that Vasyok wasn't coming. I waited for him for another ten minutes or so, but I knew that he wouldn't come, and he didn't.

" 'Inka, he didn't come,' I said.

" 'What?'

" 'Vasyok didn't show up.'

" 'Congratulations. That's the second one that stood you up.'

"She sat with the jar of cream in her hands. She looked ugly, I noted with satisfaction. In her droopy nightgown, with dabs of white cream all over her face—still bright pink after the shower. Her eyes looked really tiny without makeup.

"The next night it was Inka's turn to go on a date. She came back really late. I was already in bed, leafing through *The Arabian Nights* but unable to concentrate. Inka looked tired and sulky. She pulled her nightgown out from under her pillow, grabbed a towel, and went straight to the shower without saying a word to me. Then finally the water stopped, I heard the screech of the rusty knob, the angry rustle of the shower curtain, and Inka's heavy steps in the hall. She was wearing a nightgown and her hair was gathered in a ponytail. She carried her jeans, her shirt, and her underwear in a pile and threw them into her laundry bag, not bothering to separate them. That was not like her. I asked how her date went, but she only said 'Ah.' She plopped onto her bed and took a jar with face cream from her drawer.

"And then I noticed that Inka was crying. She didn't want me to see; she would jerk her face up so that the tears wouldn't fall. I sat next to her on her bed and said, 'Inka?' She pushed her face against my shoulder and said that she'd dumped Andrey because he was a pig. 'What did he do?' I asked. She shook her head and said that she didn't want to talk about it. We sat like that in silence. I was stroking her hair. Then she whispered, 'My period started.' I asked, 'What?' 'My period started while I was with Andrey. I didn't even notice until he put his hand down there. He said it was disgusting,' and she started to sob. I hugged her, thinking about Kostik and Vasyok, and how they stood me up. Then I thought about Danya and started to sob too.

"The next morning Vasyok wasn't at his usual station. A scrawny guy with thin red ears stood ladling kasha at the counter. Apparently, he was new at this job. He didn't know that you were supposed to stir kasha before ladling—the first portions came out too thin, and the last portions came out too thick. And also he didn't know how to hold the ladle, he tipped it over too quickly, and kasha spilled over the bowls, and slid down the edges onto the tray. He didn't flirt or talk to the counselors. In fact, he avoided making even the slightest eye contact with us.

"'Hey, where is Vasyok?' Inka asked him.

"The new guy shook his head. But then Dena came up to us and said:

'Don't you know? They caught him stealing salami. I heard Vedenej yell-ing at him last night.' And she winked at me as if she knew I was the one to blame."

Ben sighed and rubbed his neck.

"So you were a femme fatale after all," he said.

"I guess I was."

"Listen, your story is making me hungry. Are you hungry?"

She nodded.

"There's a diner at the next exit, we can stop there. I can't promise you anything as exciting as stolen salami, but the food is pretty decent."

"Okay."

But about five miles before the exit, the traffic came to a halt, so suddenly that Ben barely managed to hit the brakes in time.

"What the fuck?" Ben said.

She rolled down the window and looked ahead.

"I don't know—I can't see anything. Probably an accident."

They drove closer to the source of the jam and saw a bunch of cars parked on the curb on both sides of the road. A crowd of about fifty people stood on the bank of the little pond right off the highway, with more people getting out of their cars and approaching. A group of teenage boys armed with their iPhones crossed the road right in front of their car. Lena rolled her window down and asked what was going on. One of the boys ignored her, another made a face at her, but the third smiled and said: "There's a moose in the pond, ma'am. People are snapping pictures."

"I couldn't care less about a moose," Ben muttered.

But when they drew close, the moose was still there. Munching on some grass, perfectly oblivious to the crowd. It didn't have antlers.

"Must be a female," Ben said.

"No, I think it's a male. It looks resigned."

"And that's a male quality?"

"I don't know. It just looks like a male to me."

The moose wasn't pretty. Skinny, with ribs sticking out, a dingy worn coat, strange lumpy protrusions over its eyes, and long wet strings of grass stuck to its chin. It looked like the moose was drooling. Lena felt an urge to wipe his chin. Cameras big and small (from professional to tiny iPhones) kept clicking, whirring, and clicking again. Some people even knelt down to get a better perspective. "Come on, Moosey, baby, come on, turn your beautiful face! That's a good boy!" Apparently, this woman took the resigned, oblivious, antlerless moose for a male too. On the whole, the scene reminded Lena of a press conference. A couple of greedy and excited journalists, yelling at, and snapping pictures of, their tired subject. "Mr. President," Ben said, "care to comment?"

It was then that the moose stopped eating and retreated into the depths of the woods.

"I hate moose," Ben said.

"Why?"

"I had a very unpleasant encounter with a moose when I was a child."

"What did it do to you?"

"It looked at me."

"Ooh, that is so scary!"

"Don't laugh. It was scary! My dad had taken me hiking. There were many unmarked trails around the cabin, and Dad insisted we explore all of them. I was six, I had a blister on my foot, and I kept whining. So Dad said that he'd just walk ahead and if I couldn't keep up with him, it was my problem."

"You were six and he left you behind in the woods?"

"He didn't go very far, I think he just wanted to scare me a little. So, there I was, dragging behind, crying and spreading snot all over my face. I didn't see the moose right away because I was crying, then I saw this large blurry shape moving out of the bushes, stopping right in front of me in the middle of the road. I wiped the tears off to see it better. I think I was hoping that this thing wasn't real, that it was a shadow or a cloud or something. Yet, somehow I knew that it was real and dangerous. I kept raising my head, throwing it back to see where the thing ended. And then I saw its eyes. It looked right at me. It saw me. It knew I was there. It was just as aware of me as I was of it. That was the scariest thing of all—the fact that the moose knew I was there."

"What did you do?"

"What could I possibly do? I peed in my pants. Then the moose crossed the road and went away."

"Did you call your dad?"

"I don't remember. I just remember being back at the cabin, my pants and underpants were drying outside, and I was sitting on the futon playing with my toy Indians, dressed only in a T-shirt and socks. My socks were wet too, but Dad didn't notice."

"How old was he when he died?"

"Fifty-six."

"Cancer?"

"Heart attack. It was very sudden. He'd had heart problems for a while, but he insisted they weren't serious, and he wouldn't even take his meds.

"He made his last trip to the cabin a few months before he died. He had wanted to take me, but I refused at the last moment. It was a Memorial Day weekend. I was fourteen. Dad was packing, I was carrying things to the car. Food, clothes, his new fishing gear, a new teakettle that he had bought specially for the cabin, a checkered blanket that my mother hated. Over the years, my mother had developed this habit: whenever she would do a spring cleaning, she would put together a pile of things that she'd grown to hate and offer them to my father. 'Honey,' she would say, 'these mugs are disgusting, just looking at them makes my skin crawl, why don't you take them to the cabin?' Or 'I can't stand the sight of this thermos, why don't you take it with you?' Things that she didn't particularly hate, she would just throw away.

"So, that time Dad put all our stuff in the trunk and surveyed it, and saw that my backpack wasn't there. 'Hey, where's your backpack?' he asked. I said that I wasn't going. I sat down in the rocking chair on the porch and started rocking, hoping that this nonchalant action would give me strength against Dad's rage. But he just nodded, as if he'd been waiting for this all along, and went to the car. He was backing out of our driveway onto the road, when he stopped the car—mid-turn—and got out. I was still on the porch, still rocking like an idiot. He didn't look handsome or frightening, he looked old and lost, as if his will and drive had just seeped out of him. He took a couple of steps toward me, and he raised his hand as if he was going to make a long speech with a lot of persuasive gesturing. I told myself to resist. But then he dropped his hand, turned around, got back in the car, and drove away. And the second his car disappeared from our street, I felt something break inside me. I felt like chasing after the car and begging him to take me with him. But it was too late."

A car passed them with an angry honk. Then another. Lena flinched and looked out the window.

"Ben! We're too slow," she said.

"What do you mean?"

"You're driving too slowly. All the cars are honking and passing us."

"Oh, shit, you're right. I guess I should stop talking about Dad. It's just the thought of going to the cabin brings up all these memories. Look at me. I have a whole carload of my past."

"It's the same way with me and the camp," Lena thought. She thought of her story as this pile of clunky, chunky pieces of baggage, stuffed into Ben's car along with his books, papers, and strange household objects.

ELEVEN

Soon after the exit, a village popped into view. A church. Another village. Another church. A pharmacy. A fire department. A compact shopping mall.

A diner.

The diner was empty save for two men in overalls finishing their plates of fish and chips, and a fat gloomy woman with a two-year-old squirming and kicking in his booster seat.

The waitress seated them at the dimly lit booth in the corner, which made their whole dinner seem mysterious and seedy.

"When was the last time you went to the cabin?" Lena asked.

"About two years ago. Leslie hates the cabin, almost as much as my mom did. She's been trying to persuade me to sell it for years. I guess she's right, because I hardly use it at all, but, you know, the idea of selling it pains me. I don't think I'm ready to let it go."

"Because of your dad and all those memories?"

"No, not really. Sometimes I think that the memories are better left behind. It's just that the cabin is the only place where I can be alone."

The waitress brought them two huge plates, where the sandwiches (tuna for him, roast beef for her) lay buried under piles of chips. She was a tall woman in her fifties, with red hair in braids. She didn't smile.

Ben dug out his sandwich, swept some chips off the top, and looked it over, choosing the most convenient side for a bite. Lena bit into her sandwich in the middle, making mayonnaise and tomato juice drip out of the sides.

Ben smiled and wiped some juice off her chin. Lena was suddenly overcome with affection for him.

"Am I boring you with all that talk about the cabin?"

"No, no. I'm the one who asked you."

"After Dad died, I couldn't bring myself to go to the cabin for a long time. Especially not alone. Or even with a girlfriend. I would only go with large groups of friends. We did that a lot when I was in college. We would take tents and camp out there using the cabin as a base. That way it didn't feel like returning to the cabin. For some reason, I thought that if I went there alone, I'd let the cabin get to me, and I didn't want that.

"Then when Becky turned three, I decided to go there with Becky and Erica, my ex-wife. We'd had a difficult couple of months, we had been fighting, something was clearly wrong between us, but I couldn't tell what. I thought maybe a couple of weeks in the woods would help. I'd mentioned to Erica that I had a cabin before, but I'd never suggested going there. I'd said that it wasn't livable. But this time I said, 'Let's think of it as camping.' Erica wasn't a big fan of camping, but she was surprisingly enthusiastic about the cabin. She gasped when she saw it. She climbed out of the car and laughed: 'Beautiful! So beautiful!' She said she'd had no idea it would be so beautiful. How could I have described it as such a dreary place? How could I have hidden it from her? When everything was so poetic and wonderful?"

Lena took a sip of her coffee and looked around. The little boy had finally managed to wiggle out of his seat and was now parked in his mother's lap, happily eating French fries off his mother's plate, dunking them in his Coke from time to time. "Oh, come on, Brandon," the woman kept saying. "No, stop. You're asking for it. Yes, you are! You're pushing it, Brandon."

Ben kept talking. He was completely engrossed in his story now.

As if he was transported into the past and was talking to her from there. Lena thought she could even see his younger self in his features. Strangely, this made her feel closer to him.

"Yes, that first day at the cabin was perfect. We had breakfast by the campfire. We made orange juice using that juicer that Erica had given me on my birthday. Erica took Becky for a walk, and she kept gushing about every little chipmunk that ran past. She made us pasta on the stove ('Look! I'm like a Stone Age housewife!'), and after lunch she took Becky to splash in the lake. I watched them from the porch. Becky was wearing Erica's big floppy hat. You couldn't see her head or shoulders, just her tiny arms and legs, and her skinny bottom in bunched-up underpants, so fragile that it almost broke your heart. Erica was wearing a black swimsuit. Her body was soft, her skin very pale, the wind made her blond hair brush over the mole on her back. I wasn't sure if I was still in love with her, but she was my wife. She was the closest person to me in the whole world.

"'Isn't it wonderful?' Erica kept asking Becky, and Becky squealed in delight. She kept turning and waving at me, holding her hat with her hand. 'Daddy, come swim with us!' But I felt perfectly content just watching them from the porch.

"Later that night Erica snuggled up to me in bed and said that this was what happiness was. Happiness was peace. Happiness was having a husband and a child. Happiness was going back to nature."

"She really talked like that?" Lena asked.

"Oh, yes, she did. Much worse than that actually. But back then I didn't see anything wrong with it. Didn't notice what a phony she was. Erica—so beautiful, so smart, so refined. And then she started telling me how perfect I was and how much she loved me, how she knew every little thing on my body by heart ('Do you want me to recite all your birthmarks with my eyes closed?'), and how she loved my smell, and my taste ('But, you do have a very distinctive taste, honey') and how right it felt when I entered her, how my penis was exactly the right shape and size for her, and how 'right' and 'familiar' were more important than anything else. Then she recited some poetry, and then she started to sob, and she sobbed for hours and wouldn't tell me why. Finally, she said, 'I'm crying because I'm happy.'

"It turned out that Erica had been having an affair for the whole year before that, and she had just broken up with her lover a week before we went to the cabin. She was scared and lonely. She was bitterly miserable. She was clinging to me for protection. She practically begged me to find a way to persuade her that she was going to be okay."

Lena stopped eating and was staring at Ben.

"How do you know all that?" she asked.

"I didn't know any of it before she left me. I didn't even suspect. But after she left me, I kind of put together all the details, and I was amazed that I hadn't guessed earlier."

"But how do you know exactly how she felt? That she was scared and lonely and clinging to you for protection?"

"I figured it out, once I saw the whole picture. I did know Erica pretty well, after all."

Lena pressed the cold water glass to her forehead. She thought about Vadim going through the same pain over her infidelity. She even imagined him telling somebody their story, using the exact same expressions as Ben.

"What's wrong? Are you upset?" Ben asked.

"No, no, I'm fine. Please, go on. Go back to the cabin. I mean to the story."

"The next morning Erica slept late. I made some breakfast for Becky, we went for a walk, then a swim. I had already started preparing lunch when Erica woke up. The first thing she said to me was that she hated the shirt I was wearing. 'Want some coffee?' I asked.

"She sat at the table cradling her mug, rocking in her chair, staring at my shirt. 'I positively hate that shirt,' she said. 'You look weak and slouchy in that shirt, and I've told you this many times. Now, why did you have to wear it?' Becky climbed into her lap and said, 'No, Mommy, Daddy looks very good, very pretty in this shirt.' Erica hugged Becky, looked at me, and said that she was sorry. Then she started to cry."

Lena felt another pang of recognition. Just before this trip she had had an argument with Vadim that started with a sweater. Her favorite old sweater. "Why you insist on wearing that thing is beyond me!" he said. "Don't you see that it's way too tight?"

"Are you sure you're okay?" Ben asked.

"Yes, yes, I'm fine."

He continued.

"It went like that for the rest of the day, a total shift from the day before. Whatever I did or didn't do irritated the hell out of Erica. She would yell at me, she would nag me, I would yell back at her, and then either she or I would get scared and apologize. Toward nighttime, Becky grew listless and started to complain about an earache. She was burning up. We locked up the cabin, got in the car, and started to drive back home. The roads were dark and empty. In a couple of hours, it started to rain. Becky whimpered in the back seat. And Erica, who sat in the front seat, because riding in the back seat made her vomit, kept shushing her from the front seat, and failing that, screamed that it was my fault that Becky had gotten sick, because we had gone swimming in the morning, when the water was still cold, and that I 'always, always, always, ruined everything.'"

Ben paused and took a few bites of his sandwich. A piece of tomato fell off Ben's fork and landed on his chest, leaving a tomato-mayonnaise stain that he sloppily blotted with a napkin. He was staring at his food, but he looked as if he was having trouble focusing.

"We stayed together for a couple of years after that. But the rest of our marriage was pretty much like that weekend at the cabin. Erica would try to be nice to me, then she would get bored, then she would get angry, then she would get depressed. And then she ran away with another lover, leaving Becky to me. I didn't even feel rage or jealousy. What tortured me the most was shame. We lived in this small university town, where everybody knew each other. And I couldn't go out to the store without somebody asking about Erica. In a perfectly benign way. 'How's Erica?' 'Where's Erica? We haven't seen her in a long time.' 'Say hello to Erica.' 'I have something I need to discuss with Erica, would you ask her to call me?' And I thought that everybody knew what was going on, and that they were all secretly laughing at me. And in a while I started to wish that everybody suspected that I had killed Erica, because this would be better than their knowing that I was a pathetic deceived husband. Then I was offered a job in Boston. You can't imagine how happy I was to take it and move."

The waitress came with the dessert menu, but they didn't want anything and just asked for some coffee to go. They were already by the door when they heard a loud "Brandon! I told you this would happen!" Little Brandon had choked on a piece of French fry, and the mother lay him facedown across her knees and whacked him on the back with her fist, and after the French fry was out, slapped his butt several times.

Ben rolled his eyes and asked the waitress for their bill.

"I'm actually looking forward to the rest of your story," Ben said when they got to the car.

"Thank you!"

"No, seriously. It's like a welcome routine now. We go somewhere, we take a break from your story, then we come back to the car, and you start off where you stopped. I remember feeling like that when I was a child. I would be reading a book, a long attention-grabbing one, like *The Count of Monte Cristo*, and I would have to leave—my mother would send me to a store, I'd have classes—but I would be thinking of the book waiting for me at home, and when I finally got back, I wouldn't even open the book right away; I would look at it and stroke the pages, trying to prolong the anticipation. Have you ever felt like that?"

"Sure."

"Well, that's how I feel. You know what?"

"What?"

"I'll be sorry when the story is over."

Lena couldn't help but feel a jolt of pain. The camp story will be over sooner or later. As will the story of Lena and Ben. If only she could learn some of Scheherazade's storytelling magic and make it last.

TWELVE

"The third week of July brought three new experiences to the camp: the heat wave, the lambada, and the landing of the UFOs. There was no doubt in my mind that all three were connected.

"The heat wave came stealthily, pretending to be something pleasant at first. One Friday morning Inka and I went out on the porch and noticed that our breathing didn't produce white clouds as usual. 'Huh,' Inka said, 'nice!' and took off her sweater. Small kids were allowed to go outside in shorts and tank tops, we counselors wore the teeniest tops, mosquitoes seemed to have dropped dead overnight, and the air filled with the smell of heated pine needles, smothered grass, and over-ripe wild strawberries.

"'Are they going to open the pool?' Sveta asked.

"'They'd have to fill it with water first,' Inka said.

"And then Sasha Simonov said they couldn't open the pool, because it served as a landing pad for the aliens, and they were expecting aliens soon.

"'What are you talking about?' Inka asked. To me it just sounded like the usual Sasha nonsense, but Inka seemed genuinely interested.

"Other kids joined in the conversation, providing us with necessary alien-related info. Last year the aliens came twice. One looked like a big garden hose. They didn't do much. They landed. They stayed for an hour or two and took off. When aliens try to take you, always scream, because they can't stand high sounds. Or you can spray them with water. Just splashing water on them won't help. You have to spray them.

"Inka laughed and shook her head and said, 'Bullshit.'

"After lunch we took the kids to wade in the pond. On the map the pond appeared to be a tiny smudge of black paint. But in reality it was large, shallow, and green, overgrown with weeds and water lilies, with some irises and forget-me-nots by the banks. The kids dropped their things to the ground, kicked off their shoes, and rushed right into the water, squealing and pushing each other.

" 'Paradise on earth,' Inka said, and lay down right on the grass, not bothering to spread out the blanket. I lay down too. The grass was cool and slightly damp, and the sun on our faces felt just perfect.

" 'Listen, listen,' Inka said. She rose onto her elbow.

" *'The sun's warm and nice,*
Like the sweet sticky buns
That the kids have with milk
For their afternoon snack.' "

"I was so overcome with the sensation of perfect physical comfort that I actually liked the poem.

" 'Inka, you are a poet!' I said.

" 'Thank you,' she answered, and turned onto her stomach.

"After Inka had broken up with Andrey, we were on the same page again. We would go to the store together, we would walk to the spring, we even resumed our private book club. But we still didn't feel completely comfortable around each other. There was something that annoyed me about Inka, something that bothered me like an itch, and I couldn't understand what it was, and the fact that I couldn't understand bothered me too.

"Inka stretched and took out a book from her backpack. 'Listen,' she said, 'remember that scene with butter in *Last Tango in Paris*?'

" 'Yes.' (None of us had seen the movie, but we had just read the screenplay in the *Art of Cinema*.)

" 'What do you make of it? Do you think it is what I think it is?'

"I nodded, trying very hard to appear unflustered.

" 'I thought so,' Inka said. 'Yuck! Right?'

"I nodded.

" 'I mean it must hurt like hell, and wouldn't it, you know, be all covered in shit?'

"Even though Inka had had some sexual experience, she appeared to be as clueless as I was.

"We went on to discuss how this scene had a deeper existential meaning, as did the one about the pig and the vomit. We didn't come to any conclusion about the existential meaning, but we agreed that this was what sex was all about! Not the pig and the vomit, of course. But being capable of getting that crazy.

"Inka sighed and closed her eyes. I closed my eyes too.

"We woke up when the kids stumbled over my feet and splashed cold dirty water all over me. Inka's face was all covered in creases because she'd used the *Art of Cinema* as a pillow. My face was sore—I must have gotten sunburned. There was no water. The kids had drunk all of it and were now terribly thirsty. And hungry. Myshka said that she was so hungry that she might faint. Sasha Simonov looked as if he were actually about to faint.

" 'Get your things and start walking!' Inka said. 'You don't want to miss dinner.'

"The first half of the way, the kids walked at a crawling pace. I could barely walk myself. It felt as if we were climbing a very steep mountain, even though the ground was perfectly flat. The only thing that gave me some energy was the intense hatred of the kids. They just wouldn't shut up. Myshka was sniveling because Sveta Kozlova punched her. Alesha Pevtcov claimed that he had been bitten by a frog. Sasha Simonov was whimpering like a dog, because his stomach ached. I thought that if I heard one more complaint from somebody, I would hit him or her with an empty teakettle. Apparently, Inka felt the same, because when

Alesha said that he couldn't walk anymore because his frog-bitten butt itched, she did hit him with her kettle.

"It worked. The kids shut up and picked up their pace.

"We felt so tired, so wiped out throughout the rest of the day, that we could barely wait until bedtime, so we could just get the kids to bed, go to our room, and maybe read the *Art of Cinema* a little or just go to sleep. The second day of the heat wave fell on Friday, the day of the third dance. It had been so hot throughout the day that nobody felt like dancing, but we couldn't possibly miss the dance. And so we dragged the kids to the dance floor.

"I saw Danya and forgot about the heat and exhaustion for a second. He didn't even look at me. He stood by the fence staring ahead. Most of the people just stood by the fence, reluctant to move. Even the DJ, Volodya, seemed sluggish and bleary-eyed. So you could imagine how stunned everyone looked when Yanina took the mike from him and announced a new dance.

" 'Lambada!' "

"Lambada?" Ben asked.

"Yes, lambada. You don't know it?"

"No. What is it? Something Latin?"

"Yeah. It's like salsa, only simpler and dirtier. It was so big in Russia in the eighties! At the camp everybody went crazy over it."

"Dirtier than salsa? Sounds good."

"It's really very simple. You put your legs very far apart, bend your knees just a little, so that your spine remains straight, and you make dance steps while rocking and swirling your hips. Not your waist, or your ass, but your hips. It looks as if you're about to straddle someone."

"That is dirty!"

"I know."

"So you're saying they allowed this dirty dance at the camp with the hands-over-the-blankets policy?"

"Only because it came from Yanina herself."

"Uh-huh. Well, go on."

"Volodya hurried to put the new tape in. And then the music started and everybody seemed to come alive. Sveta Kozlova, who had been engaged in torturing Myshka—coming up to her and breathing into her face—left Myshka alone and screamed: 'Lambada! Lambada.' We all knew the tune—it had been playing on TV a lot, but nobody seemed to know how to do the dance. People kept looking at Dena—but she only shook her head.

"Yanina walked to the middle of the floor and yelled to Volodya: 'Turn it up!'

"She was dressed in a tight polyester dress covered with prints of birds, flowers, and dragonflies.

"She pressed her hand to her chest, took a deep breath, and started. She danced alone. Her legs were very short, and she spread them very far apart, which looked really indecent, almost obscene, but also oddly beautiful. She rocked and swirled her hips really hard, but she managed to make her movements really smooth and elegant. But the most amazing thing was the expression on her face. She looked shy and nervous like a young girl in love. And sometimes she would blush and smile as if at an imaginary partner.

"All eyes were on her.

"I looked at Danya. He moved away from the fence and was staring at Yanina as if hypnotized.

"The song came to an end. Yanina stopped, stomped her foot on the floor, and snapped her fingers. Everybody erupted in applause."

Lena's phone made a single plaintive beep. She started in her seat and reached to take her phone out of her bag.

"Don't worry," Ben said. "It just means that we've gone out of range. Now we are officially cut off from the world."

She looked at her phone—there were no bars. Instead of feeling nervous that she was cut off from civilization, out in the wilderness with a man she barely knew, Lena just smiled. She felt as if the loss of connection made it easier to breathe somehow.

A few miles past Bangor they exited I-95 onto a smaller road. There were just a few cars going in their direction; all of them with Maine license plates, most of them pickups sporting large dogs sitting either in the back or in the passenger seat, looking contentedly out the window. The scenery became sparser, with open meadows, uncut grass, occasional farms surrounded by thin low woods.

"We'll need to stop at one place," Ben said, "to get the keys. There's this guy, Mike, who's been keeping an eye on the cabin while I'm away."

The road seemed to go on forever, but finally they saw a trail of wood shavings on the road and the figure of a life-sized plywood moose, followed by a pack of bunny-sized plywood bears, and right after that a big clearing with a one-story house, very small, very neat, painted bluish-gray, surrounded by more animal figures, big and small. To the right of the house was a large shed with a workbench in front and a variety of half-finished wooden animals on the grass.

Mike's car wasn't in the driveway, though. They knocked on the door of the house, but there was no answer. There wasn't anybody in the shed either, but they saw a big box on the ground with a slit on the top and a handwritten sign: "Be back soon—leave your orders here."

Ben groaned. "I told him I was coming. He said he'd be here all day."

He took out his phone to try Mike's number, but of course there was no service. "We'll have to wait," he said.

They walked behind the shed along the little path that led to the thin birch grove.

Ben took his jacket off, spread it on the grass and sat down, leaving a space for her. Lena sat down next to him. The setting sun lent a rosy glow to Mike's house, to all the wooden moose and bunnies, to Ben's face. She wanted to touch him, which shouldn't have been difficult considering what they had already done, but for some reason she couldn't. She wondered if Ben felt the same.

"Time for the next installment of your story," he said.

"Okay. Where was I?"

"You were talking about the heat wave and how it made everyone engage in some sort of pornodance."

"Oh, yes. Lambada! Okay, so, the next day it was even hotter in the camp. We could barely get up in the morning. Throughout the day everybody talked about the heat wave, how stuffy it was at night, and how sweaty we were, and how stinky our clothes were, and what were the best foods to eat when it was hot, and how awful the soldiers must feel in their uniforms, and all the possible ways to stay cool—actually there was just one—to stay in the shade and splash yourself with cold water from time to time.

"The cafeteria smelled of burning fat that day. The first course was already on the tables—steaming bowls of lamb soup, dark brown with gleaming yellow circles of fat. The kids started to make gagging sounds. All those 'Yucks!' and 'Blehs!' and 'Urgghs.' They were so good at it that we missed the moment when Sasha Simonov started to throw up for real. Inka dragged him outside, but it was too late, and Yanina's aunt came and mopped up the vomit, cursing and looking at me as if I'd been the one to make the mess.

"'Are they kidding?' Inka said when we saw that they were serving meat dumplings as the second course. I don't know if this was Sasha's fault or not, but nobody wanted dumplings. Most of the kids sat breaking them up with their forks, until Alesha Pevtcov discovered that dumplings were just perfect for tossing, especially if you put them on the tip of a fork, and hit on the dumpling-free end of the fork. Other kids followed suit, and it caught on with the kids from the other units. I exchanged panicky glances with Inka—we had absolutely no strength to deal with a food fight, and then, by a stroke of luck, Alesha hit Sveta on the face. She charged forward, grabbed Alesha by the collar and said that if he threw one more dumpling, she would take the whole pile of them from the kitchen and shove them down his throat, one by one, until he died. Alesha turned red and started to cry. Other kids froze. Even the kids at the adjacent table grew silent and stopped throwing dumplings. I couldn't think of anything to say or do, but Inka could. 'Shut up and stand up!' she yelled. 'We're going back to the unit.' Her face glowed with power. Or maybe her face just glowed because of the heat, but I still admired her."

Ben yawned and lay down on the grass.

Lena fell silent.

"No, no, don't stop," he said. "I love listening to you."

"Are you?"

"Am I what?"

"Listening?"

"Of course! Do you mind if I close my eyes, though?"

Lena smiled.

"When they got back to their units, Myshka asked Inka what she did when she went on a date.

"'Not much,' Inka said. 'We walk, we talk.'

"'Do the boys kiss you?'

"'Shut up, Myshka.'

"'So they do. And what do they do then?'

"'Nothing.'

"'Nothing? Really? Don't they fuck you? Not even a little?'"

Ben stirred and mumbled, "Yeah, I was wondering the same thing."

"And then there was the performance of Sveta Kozlova.

"I was in the girls' bedroom stripping the beds, when Inka ran in choking with laughter. 'Open the window, quick, you've got to see this, Sveta is doing Yanina!'

"There was a circle of kids by the porch. Sveta was in the center apparently waiting for a cue. Then, Alesha opened his mouth very wide and began to sing the lambada. Just 'A . . . Aaaa . . . 'Aaa . . . a'aa . . . aa'a' like this, but he carried the tune well. And Sveta pressed her hand to her chest and sighed deeply, exactly like Yanina did. Then she began to move. The resemblance was simply amazing. She even looked like Yanina a little. The same beefy little body, the same flush on her plump cheeks. At the end she raised her arms up just like Yanina did, only Sveta didn't pretend that she did it to snap her fingers. She put her arms in a circle and moved them up and down as if she was hugging somebody.

"'Yasha, my darling, kiss me, kiss me,' she said, and made some loud smooching sounds to the delight of the kids.

"'Who is Yasha?' I asked Inka.

" 'Don't you get it?'

" 'No.'

" 'Yasha . . . Yakov . . . Ring a bell?'

" 'No! It can't be!'

"But Inka gave me a meaningful nod.

"There was only one Yasha at our camp. The camp director. Yakov Petrovich Vedeneev. I started to laugh. Yanina and Vedenej? No, this couldn't be true.

" 'Oh, Yasha! I love you so much,' Sveta continued. 'Fuck me. Fuck me, please. Just a little bit.' 'Wait, Yanina Ivanovna, wait, let me get it out of my pants, it must be stuck.' "

Lena looked at Ben. She expected him to laugh, but he only smiled without opening his eyes.

"Inka flung the window open and yelled that Sveta must stop and shut up. Amazingly, Sveta stopped right away. She must have felt satisfied that she had done enough damage.

"Later that day, when we went to the laundry room with the pile of dirty sheets, we asked Galina if there was any truth to Sveta's playacting.

" 'Come on, girls,' Galina said, 'Vedenej and Yanina? They are husband and wife. They don't exactly publicize it, but everybody knows that.'

"Nadezhda peeked from behind the shelves.

" 'Vedenej and Yanina? I can't believe you didn't know!'

"More counselors were coming in with their laundry and joining in the discussion. It turned out that everybody who had been to this camp before knew the story. Some knew just parts of the story, but others eagerly supplied missing links, as well as their opinions on the story. It went like this: a new pile of laundry unloaded onto the floor, a fresh bit of info added to the story. But the counselors didn't leave after they dumped their laundry, they stayed to listen to what the others would say, and to correct them in case their info or their opinion was wrong. It seemed like the story expanded along with the pile of laundry on the floor. And the voices got louder and louder trying to outshout the drone of washing machines and each other.

"The story went like this.

" 'They met here six or seven years ago. Vedenej was married then. You should've seen how Yanina was throwing herself at him! Well, Vedenej used to be very into her as well. Must be the sex stuff. Yanina must have done something—you know—that a decent woman wouldn't do.' (*Last Tango in Paris*! Butter! flashed through my mind.)

" 'But when the summer was over, Vedenej called it quits and went back to Moscow to his wife. He thought he got off easy. Right! Yanina looked up his home address—pulled some serious strings at the Ministry—and went straight to his apartment. Nobody knows what she did, whether she enticed him or threatened him, but the fact is that he divorced his wife and married Yanina. The main problem is that Vedenej is getting sick of Yanina now. He comes to the camp, he wants to fuck somebody else—there are so many temptations, Yanina watches him all the time.'

"And then one woman said: 'I think he still loves Yanina. If he cheats on her, it doesn't mean that he doesn't love her.' And then she started to cry.

"Inka and I exchanged glances.

"Love seemed to be this grim, hard, confusing thing."

Lena looked down at Ben, apprehensive of his reaction. He was fast asleep. She lay down next to him. There was a little leaf stuck to his forehead. She gently removed it and closed her eyes.

That night at the camp, the counselors' room got so hot that Inka and Lena could barely breathe.

Finally, Lena got up and opened the window, letting in a feeble trickle of warm air and a swarm of mosquitoes revived and seemingly refreshed after their day of rest. "You idiot!" Inka yelled. Lena shut the window, but it was too late, mosquitoes buzzed and zoomed in on them, and they swatted at the annoying insects with the *Art of Cinema* until most of them were dead.

"I'm taking off my nightgown," Inka said. Lena took off hers too.

"You have a nice body," Inka said, "I wouldn't have guessed."

"You too," Lena said.

She couldn't help but look at Inka's breasts. Discreetly, she hoped. They were large and low-slung, and looked like a woman's breasts rather than a young girl's breasts. They looked serious. Lena liked Inka's nipples, though. They were small and pale-yellow. She imagined that they were extremely tender and sensitive to touch. Not that she wanted to touch them. She did think about touching Inka's stomach—she thought it was okay to want to touch a person's stomach as opposed to a person's breasts. Inka had squashy folds over her panty line. Lena wondered what it would be like to press her face into her stomach and sink into its soft warmth. She never dared to imagine what was below Inka's panty line.

"So, do you think they really do it?" she asked Inka.

"Who?"

"Yanina and Vedenej?"

"They are married. They must be doing it."

"Can you even visualize it? I can't. How do they go about it?"

"I think they come to his office at night."

"No, I mean what does she do? How does she make him want it?"

"Don't men want it all the time?"

"Well, they work close by in the headquarters. She probably comes into his office and unbuttons her blouse and says: 'Oh, oh, isn't it hot today, my dear Yasha.'"

"Uh-huh. And he stares at her tits and says: 'Oh, yes, Yanina Iva-novna, it's certainly hot today.'"

"And she says:

"'Oh, give me the kisses of your mouth,'
(How does it go in the Song of Songs?)
'For your sweet loving . . .'
(Yeah, yeah, sweet loving!)
'For your sweet loving is better than wine,
Your juices are fragrant,*

Your essence pours out like oil,
This is why all the young women want you.'

"And he says:

" *'Your lips, my bride, drip honey,*
Honey and milk are under your tongue,
And your clothes hold the scent of Lebanon.' "

"What's the scent of Lebanon?"
"I don't know, some kind of rose water?"
"Rose water? Yanina smelling like rose water? No, no, it should go like this:

" *'Your lips, my bride, drip borscht,*
Beets and cabbage are under your tongue,
And your clothes hold the scent of salami.'

"And she says:

" *'And your cock is like a tower of Babel!' "*

"And he says, 'Hm, Yanina Ivanovna, really?'
"And she says: 'Oh, yes, yes. In fact, it's even bigger than the tower of Babel. I love it more than anything in the world! I love it more than that salami we've been stealing from the kids.'
" 'More than salami? Really? All right, Yanina Ivanovna, just you wait!' And then he jumps over his desk."

And the next thing Lena knew, Inka was on her bed on top of her, and they were rolling around laughing and squealing. Inka was so soft all over. Her breasts pushed against Lena's ribcage and they were really soft. Lena grabbed her on the back and her back was kind of soft too. Inka was soft, but so very strong. Heavier and stronger than Lena. Lena felt that Inka could do whatever she wanted with her. And she was pressing too hard and it became hard to breathe, and Lena squealed "Inka, let me go!" If she had said "Yanina Ivanovna, let me go," she probably wouldn't have. But she called her Inka and that brought them back to reality. Inka moved away from Lena and surveyed the scene. The two of them on the bed. Two girls. One chubby and one skinny. One wearing light blue panties. The other one wearing white panties with small flowers on them. Both topless, red-faced, and disheveled. Inka jumped off the bed and went to put on her nightgown. Lena put on her nightgown too.

They went to sleep facing in opposite directions.

In twenty minutes or so, Ben shifted and opened his eyes. Lena smiled at him. The rosy glow around them had faded, and the thin gray dusk settled in, not yet ready to get really dark.

"Did I sleep?" he asked.

Lena nodded.

"Did I fall asleep in the middle of your story?"

"Yes, you did."

"Oh, that's bad."

"I was just about to tell you how Inka and I almost had sex."

He sat up and stared at Lena. "You and Inka had sex?"

"We came close, yes, but we got scared at the last moment."

"Tell me what happened."

"We fooled around. That was it."

"You fooled around, huh?"

Ben rubbed his forehead and looked away.

"What?" Lena asked.

"Has it ever occurred to you that it could've been Inka?" Ben asked.

"What could've been Inka?"

"The one who made the soldiers disappear?"

"How? Why?"

"Suppose she was in love with you?"

"Inka? No!"

"No, no. Don't dismiss my idea. Let's go back to the beginning. She wanted that double date with you and the first guy, right?"

"Kostik."

"And you couldn't understand why, right?"

"Yes, but—"

"No, wait, listen. And she tried to ruin the date for you, right? She said that you looked like a squirrel or ate like a squirrel or something?"

Lena was surprised that he even remembered the squirrel.

"And she tried to drag you into the woods with her every chance she got."

"We went with the kids!"

"And you were spending every free minute you got just lying around and reading dirty books."

"Those books were classics!"

"And she tried to give you a hint about your secret admirer!"

The secret admirer? Could Inka possibly mean herself? No, that was ridiculous. Or was it? Anyway, Lena didn't want to get into it with Ben. She needed some time to think this new angle over on her own.

"Come on, stop it," she said to Ben. "What about you, by the way?"

"What?"

"Have you been with a man?"

"No. It just doesn't interest me at all."

"Not even when you were a boy?"

"No. Well, once, when I was thirteen. We spent a weekend with my parents' friends down in Cape May. I had to share a room with their son—he was about my age. I don't know how it happened. We were in his room. We started to fight—not for real—just, you know, pushing each other. And then our dicks were out—I honestly don't remember who was the first to get his dick out. They were stiff like rolling sticks, and pointing straight up, and we kept touching each other and laughing like crazy. But that was it. We didn't have sex."

A rustle in the tree above them made Lena scream.

"What's wrong?"

"There was a squirrel. I'm sorry! I'm terrified of squirrels. When I look at a squirrel, I always imagine that it will jump on me and start clawing at my face. It's insane."

"Oh, don't worry, you're perfectly sane, and your fear isn't irrational at all."

"What? What do you mean?"

"Squirrels are vicious. Not many people know that, but they do attack humans. But only if you disturb them during mating."

"Really?" She peered at the top of the tree and moved away from the trunk and closer to Ben.

"Yeah."

"How do we know if they're mating?"

"Oh, they make a very specific sound, it's easy to hear. The male and the female climb to the top of two different trees and stare at each other, screeching and shaking like crazy. Imagine a clothes dryer gone wild. Then they leap toward each other and the male has to penetrate the female in midair. The whole act lasts less than a second."

"In midair? But how—"

"Takes a lot of training. I heard that younger squirrels miss a lot."

She stared at him. He looked completely serious except for those tiny crinkles at the corners of his eyes. After a moment, she laughed. "I can't believe I bought it!"

"You see," he said, smiling and stroking her leg with a blade of grass. "I was a scrawny sickly teenager, not particularly good at sports, so I spent most of my childhood reading books about faraway countries and rare animals. I especially enjoyed them if there was a description of how animals fucked."

"And if there wasn't any description, you would make it up?"

"No, I just tried to guess how it was for them. I would imagine myself in their place and think what I would've done."

"You would've leapt from the top of a tree?"

"Try me!"

"No!"

And the next second he was on top of her. Bearing down on her, squashing her, pressing into her stomach.

///////////////////////

By the time a pickup pulled into the driveway, it had gotten chilly and dark. A short plump messy-haired woman wearing white sweatpants and a blue jean shirt got out of the car.

"Marty!" Ben said.

She looked at Ben, gasped, squeezed Ben in a bear hug, and started to squeal. "Ben, Ben, Ben, Benny, Ben!" Her face turned bright pink under the wisps of her gingery hair.

Ben smiled and said: "Marty, hey!" Then turned to Lena. "Lena—Marty. Marty—Lena. Marty's Mike's wife." Marty shook Lena's hand and whispered to Ben over her shoulder, "So, Benny, Leslie's out?" He shook his head, and Marty shrugged. "I thought I'd ask." She exuded warmth and the sweet smell of sweat, flowers, and cinnamon buns.

"Where's Mike?" Ben asked as they followed Marty to the front door.

"He had to make a last-minute delivery. Not sure when he'll be back."

"You have a beautiful house," Lena said.

"Well, yeah. I don't really care. My husband takes care of it. Puts in flowers and stuff."

"Marty, what's with the trolls?" Ben asked.

Marty rolled her eyes. "That's Mike, Ben. That's his new business. He carves all these stupid figurines. Plywood moose, plywood bears, bunnies, loons—whatnot. And it sells! I don't know what kind of idiot would want to buy a plywood moose when we have too many live ones around here, but apparently there are plenty of idiots. He even gets mail orders now."

She led them into the kitchen, sat them at the large table by the wall, and said that she'd run upstairs to freshen up and then they'd have some coffee. But before she did that, she hugged Ben again. Lena thought that she caught some strange intimacy in their gestures.

"Did you sleep with her?" Lena asked after Marty had gone upstairs.

For a moment Ben looked surprised at Lena's forthrightness, then nodded. "A couple of times. Years ago. Look, we've known each other for so long—it would've been wrong and almost impolite if I hadn't."

"I see."

Three ideas crossed Lena's mind, one after another, or perhaps all at the same time. That Marty liked to squeal in bed, that she liked to move around a lot, and that her favorite position was doggy-style. She felt an instant surge of jealousy.

"Does Mike know about you two?"

"No, of course not. He's a great guy and they have a great marriage. Four kids. Four kids, can you believe that?"

Marty came down wearing a white T-shirt and blue jeans. She had also put on some lip gloss and sprinkled herself with perfume—sharp and sour, not suiting her at all.

"Where are you from?" she asked Lena as the water in the coffee-maker started to gurgle.

"Originally from Russia, but I live in Boston now."

"Russia! I was wild about Russia when I was in college. I went to college, you know. Down there in Portland. I had to drop out when I got pregnant, but still I went to college. My husband never did. But my kids are all going to college, mark my words."

"How old are they?"

"Sixteen, fourteen, and the twins are eleven."

Marty took a plate with leftover strawberry pie from the fridge and cut a slice for Lena. The crust was crumbly and hard, and the filling too sweet and gooey.

"Russia! Did you like it there? But of course you did, that's your home! How I wanted to go there. To Moscow and St. Petersburg. Such a great crazy country. So what do you think about Putin?"

"Putin? I don't really think about Putin."

"He puts on airs, acts like he's this tough guy, but he's a sleazy little jerk, don't you think?"

"Yes, kind of."

"I liked Yeltsin. He was like an older Bill Clinton. Bill Clinton is my favorite president. My husband hates his guts, though. He's a Republican. I don't understand how anyone with half a brain could be a Republican. And you know what, I loved, loved Gorbachev. Such a sweet, smart man."

Lena said that she loved Gorbachev too. And Bill Clinton.

"Are you married?" Marty asked.

Lena nodded.

"Kids?"

Lena nodded again. Marty reached and patted her hand in a compassionate gesture, then leaned close to whisper something, but then changed her mind.

She kissed Lena on the cheek when they parted. Sticky lip gloss kiss, and the smell of her perfume seemed to creep after them into the car.

Thirteen

Their next stop was at a supermarket to get the necessary provisions for the cabin.

Lena felt ridiculous strolling down the supermarket aisles with Ben.

Normally, she went to the supermarket with her husband and kids. She hated supermarkets, so each time she would devise ways to spend as little time there as possible. She would make a list and then tear it in four pieces and give each member of the family a piece—some easy items for her younger son. When making the list, she tried to put the foods in the order of supermarket aisles, so there wouldn't be darting back and forth. "We get a cart each, and then we meet by the cashier in ten minutes and put all the food together," she would say. She tried to make it sound like fun, like a scavenger hunt, but she always looked so annoyed that it would ruin the cheerful mood.

And once they got to the store, her strategy never worked. Each of them would become distracted by various items that weren't on the list and forget about the ones that were. Misha would leaf through the issues of *National Geographic* and Pokemon guides in the magazine section. Borya would concentrate on discreetly stocking up on junk food. Vadim would get lost among the latest models of grills, even though he'd never grilled anything in his life. And she would be glued to the

shelves in the International Foods section, reading the cooking instructions on the packages of Thai noodles and curry sauces. And then each
of them would rush to the cashiers to look for the others and, not finding them there, dart back and forth among the aisles.

"So, what are we getting?" Ben asked.

"I don't know. Anything. I don't care."

Ben sighed.

"Okay, so you won't help me. Well, let's just walk down the aisles
and grab what we think we need."

They bought coffee, bread, apples, cheese, salad mix, lemons, water,
eggs, oranges, olive oil, a pound of potatoes, foil, paper towels, tissues,
a flashlight, and biscotti. Then she ran into the pharmacy next door,
where she bought Excedrin Migraine, mosquito repellent, and a pack
of Pirate's Booty cheese puffs—those she bought automatically, simply
because she was used to getting them for her kids every time she went
to a big pharmacy. Ben emerged from a liquor store with a bottle of
expensive tequila, looking unsure of his choice and possibly even embarrassed by it.

Their purchases looked even more ridiculous as they were putting
them in the small trunk of his car. Bigger things, smaller things, bottles.
Or perhaps, it was they who looked ridiculous, engaged in this domes-
tic activity. Ben leaned over his trunk, contemplating the most secure
position for a carton of eggs. He had to move the boxes with his books
and utensils to make the groceries fit. Past making space for the urgent
needs of the present. The juicer fell out. He picked it up and shoved it
back.

Lena climbed into her seat and felt strangely comfortable, at home.
After all this travel the shape and surface of the seat felt familiar and
pleasing, and even the mess on the back seat had a homey feel about it.
She thought that Ben's car was starting to feel more comfortable to her
than the one parked by her home in Brookline.

Lena realized that she was also starting to feel just as comfortable in
the world of her story. Telling it in Ben's car now seemed like the most
natural thing in the world.

"The next Monday after that lambada weekend, Yanina was late for the morning assembly. She arrived in the middle of the roll call, but stood apart from the others, leaning against the flagpost. She looked tired, and she didn't walk up onto the platform even for her announcement.

" 'Something horrible happened last night. I want all the counselors and staff in my office after breakfast. Take the kids back to your units— we'll dispatch soldiers to watch them—and come to my office right away.'

"And of course, this was the most exciting breakfast ever. Everybody kept whispering and exchanging ideas. Counselors asked kitchen help. Older kids asked younger kids. Younger kids asked counselors. Kitchen help asked the kids. Everybody had heard something, but nobody knew anything for sure. There were hundreds of different ideas, the most popular being these:

"1. A kid ran away.
2. A kid ran away and was killed.
3. Gorbachev was killed.
4. The U.S. finally dropped that nuclear bomb on us.
5. Vedenej ran away with Natasha the nurse (neither had been seen at the assembly).
6. Vedenej ran away with ten boxes of salami and caviar.
7. Aliens came.

"For once, we couldn't wait to get to Yanina's office. By the time Inka and I got there, all of the chairs were taken. Many people crowded by the walls. Inka and I stood by the door next to Nadezhda. Yanina sat slumped behind her desk. I thought that she seemed both intimidating and frightened. She didn't say anything for a while, waiting for everybody to arrive. There was a single window in the room. It was closed. Right when I started to sweat myself, the room filled with a strong stench of sweat. For a moment or two I worried that I was the one who stank, before I realized the other girls were sweating too, as well as Yanina herself.

" 'Guys,' she finally said. 'Last night, two people from our camp were seen engaged in a perverse sexual act.'

"The room reacted with a collective gasp. I was convinced that Yanina was referring to what Inka and I had done on my bed the night before. I stared at my knees, and I thought that Yanina must be pointing in our direction, and everybody was turning to look at us, and in a second she would ask us to step forward. I thought maybe I could squeeze past Nadezhda and out the door. I felt the blood draining out of my entire body and going to my head to thump there in heavy merciless strokes. I peeked at Inka and saw that she was thinking the exact same thing. She was staring at her hands, her face bright pink.

" 'One of the counselors . . .' Yanina continued (and I thought yes, yes, one of the counselors, not two, Inka started it, she jumped onto my bed, it wasn't my fault!). 'One of the counselors saw the couple in the woods by the pond. Neither was identified.'

"Yanina looked each of us over.

" 'Look at her,' Nadezhda whispered. 'The eyes of a she-wolf. She is looking for her. Trying to sniff her out.'

" 'Do you think it was Vedenej, with someone?' I whispered back.

" 'Oh, yeah. At least Yanina thinks so, or why would she make such a fuss?'

"She concluded the meeting by reading the list of urgent measures, which ranged from fixing the fence separating the camp territory from the woods to an even stricter hands-over-the-blankets policy.

"Volodya said that he had a question. 'What was the perverse act?'

"Somebody snickered. But Yanina just glared at Volodya.

"She looked us over and said: 'You know, you might think that sex is something funny, but it can ruin your life. It can!' Her voice broke when she said that. She looked as if she was close to tears. The expression on her face reminded me of my mother's, the way she had looked the whole year before she threw my father out. The two sharp lines that would sprout in the corners of her mouth from time to time. Years later I understood that these lines appear when you try to keep your mouth from quivering, when you try to appear tough, while feeling frightened and lost.

"It was such an enormous relief to get out of the headquarters. We were all walking down the path that led from the headquarters to the rest of the camp in silence, together but separately, as one big disjointed herd.

"But once we swerved onto the main path, and the headquarters were no longer in view, everybody stopped as if on cue.

"'Well, I guess it's clear about the guy, but who the fuck was the girl?' Svetlana asked.

"'Could be anybody,' Galina said.

"'Could be you!' Nadezhda said to her.

"'I'm happily married!'

"'Oh, right! I keep forgetting.'

"'Don't fight, girls,' Volodya said. 'And anyway, I wouldn't be so sure that the guy was Vedenej.'

"But when nobody paid any attention, he shook his head and walked away.

"The rest of us continued gossiping.

"'Listen,' Svetlana said. 'Where is Natasha?'

"Everybody looked around. Natasha wasn't there.

"'Was she at the meeting?'

"We couldn't remember.

"'But she is a nurse,' Inka said. 'She probably couldn't leave her office.'

"'Natasha? No way!' Galina said. 'She's not even that pretty.'

"'Remember Anya from last year? And that—what's her name—that really skinny girl from the year before? Were they pretty? And look at Yanina!'

"'Yeah,' Nadezhda agreed. 'Vedenej has weird taste.'

"'Anybody noticed how Natasha hangs around the phone booth every night?' Inka asked.

"'Yeah, but why would she want to call Vedenej? He's right here.'

" 'But they can't really talk, because of Yanina. So she comes to talk to him on the phone every night. He's in his office, like ten feet away from her. And he can see her in the booth through his window. Isn't it romantic?'

"But nobody had a chance to contemplate the beauty of the situation, because right at that moment we heard a blood-curdling scream. We stopped talking and froze. The scream was followed by silence—I heard nothing but the thumping of my heart.

"Everybody rushed to their units. 'It's coming from the swimming pool!' Nadezhda said, and we all ran there.

"And then a series of screams, not as bad as the first one, but still scary.

"A small crowd had already gathered by the pool. We couldn't see anything behind the backs of other people, but then somebody moved and we saw our own Myshka, squatting at the shallow part of the empty pool. She was screaming and swinging her head right and left. Inka reached to pull her out, and Myshka jumped into her arms. She was shivering.

"Later that day, after Myshka had calmed down, we managed to coax out of her what had happened. She claimed to have seen the aliens. She said she was walking back from the club with the other kids—they were watching a movie during our meeting with Yanina—and she was lagging behind, because her shoe wasn't right. Then, all of a sudden, she said she saw a round metal object swishing by. No, not like a saucer, but like a ball. She ducked her head but the object hit her on the shoulder. It vanished right after. She got scared, ran to the pool, and jumped in. The swishing ball was obviously an alien ship.

" 'Many alien ships are shaped like footballs,' Sasha Simonov confirmed with great authority. 'It was a good thing that Myshka screamed.'

" 'Why?' Inka asked.

"Sasha sighed loudly, having explained this all earlier: 'Because aliens can't stand high sounds. Their molecules fall apart. But they really appreciate music, only if it's not high-pitched. If you want to have an encounter, sing in a low voice.'

" 'Everybody knows that!' Sveta added.

"It was strange, but other than providing us with details, the kids seemed to be pretty much indifferent about the aliens. By the end of the day, even Myshka seemed to have forgotten about her encounter.

"Inka was the one who got the most excited about it.

"After lunch she went to examine the area around the pool. She came back even more excited. She didn't see anything resembling an alien soccer ball, but she saw patches of burnt grass on the edge of the woods by the pool. She could swear that the grass was freshly burnt. Then she asked if I knew that when a person had an encounter with aliens, she would usually receive a gift of special wisdom? I shook my head. I didn't know. I didn't want to know. I used to make fun of people who claimed that they saw aliens, but now I was simply annoyed, with aliens, and with Inka and her crazy interest in them.

"That night all I wanted was to go to sleep and forget about all that stuff. But Inka couldn't fall asleep for a long time. She tossed, and turned, and moaned. And of course, in the middle of the night there came a poem. Which was the longest and by far the most expressive of her poems. I still remember it.

"Aliens! Come to me.
I'm a space element.
I'm a cosmic creature.
I'm a part of the universe.
Come to me! Take me with you.
Fuck all the guys.
Who needs them.
Guys are losers.
Aliens! Take me!

"I woke up with a terrible headache and thought, 'Aliens, please, take her. And do it soon.' "

Fourteen

Ben drove deeper into the woods as the road became more crooked and narrow. The car swished past the bushes, twigs crunching under the wheels, until it swerved sharply to the right onto another dirt road that seemed even narrower and more crooked. Random patches of woods singled out by the headlights rushed at them, and then past. Coarse pine trunks, smoother birches, delicate hemlock leaves. Lena half-expected to see a goblin or a troll peeking out from behind a tree.

The car made another sharp swerve and there it was, the cabin. It stood in a partial clearing in the yellow cone of headlights, hemlock, low bushes, and tall weeds. Gray and stern, it was strangely asymmetrical. On the side facing them, there was a single window and a door with a small stoop and large rusty padlock.

They shivered as they got out of the car. It was bitterly cold, and the wind came at them in hard gusts that smelled just like snow. She cuddled up to Ben as he struggled to get his key into the right hole. He let her walk in first. It was even colder inside the cabin, and dark except for the light from the car that came through the opened door and un-washed window. Lena fumbled on the wall trying to find a light switch. "No lights," Ben said casually. "There's an oil lamp, I'll get some oil and light it."

"What do you mean, no lights?"

"The cabin doesn't have electricity."

"No electricity! Don't tell me there is no running water!"

"There is no running water." Lena thought she could see Ben smile.

"And the toilet is just the woods?"

"Oh, no. We have excellent facilities here. There's an outhouse—roomy and clean, or at least it was clean when I last saw it."

"Nice, Ben. So first you lure women here, and then you tell them that there is no toilet?"

"I warned you it was rustic." Ben's eyes glowed with amusement as he lit two lamps and put them on the table, which immediately attracted a swarm of moths. There was only one room in the cabin, with a woodstove, a table and a couple of chairs by the window, and two bookcases in the corner forming a tiny makeshift bedroom. Everything looked rough, dusty, homely and exposed. Lena found it moving.

"I love it," Lena said. "If only it weren't so cold."

"I'll start the fire in the stove," Ben said, "but it'll take a while to heat the cabin. We can make a campfire outside in the meantime. Go to the bedroom, look for something to wear—there should be plenty of old jeans. I used to be thin once, you know."

Behind the bookcases there was a futon covered with three different blankets, one checkered pattern peeking from under another. At the foot of the futon sat a row of different-sized boxes. The sign on the smallest said MAGAZINES, and the sign on the biggest said EQUIP. She peeked into the EQUIP. bin and saw a hammer, a large net, three broken umbrellas, and a ragged leather case with a thermos inside. The thermos had a white plastic knob and a blue strap. It must have been the same one that Ben and his dad used to take on their skiing trips. She reached out a finger to stroke the hard yellowed leather of the case.

The clothes were kept in a huge plastic bin with a paper sign that plainly stated CLOTHES. The clothes didn't smell musty at all. They smelled like cold, hard earth and a little like oranges. Which wasn't surprising, she thought when she found some dried-up orange peel wrapped in a sweater. Most of the sweaters were too rough and prickly.

Only one looked both soft and warm, but it had a large brown stain across the chest. All the way here Lena had been fantasizing about undressing and going to bed with Ben as soon as they got to the cabin. But it was so cold here that she wouldn't have undressed at gunpoint. She took Ben's high-waisted jeans and wore them over her leggings. She had to tie them with a string at the waist and roll them up at the hem. And she wore Ben's stained sweater over her shirt. Her reflection in the tiny mirror on the wall reminded her of herself back in Russia, putting on all these bulky warm clothes, getting ready for a school ski trip. She was simultaneously turning into Ben and into her younger self.

Outside, they sat on a rickety half-rotten bench by the campfire ring. The bench was facing the lake, but they couldn't see the water in the dark; they could only hear the heavy splashes of waves.

Ben had built a complicated structure of sticks and logs, crowned by a *Times* Business section from 1987. It took him a while to start the fire—he kept adding more and more paper, until the Business section all burned and he had to resort to Sports. That did the trick. The smaller sticks finally caught fire, and the bigger logs followed suit.

Lena shivered and moved closer to Ben.

"Perfect for a horror story, don't you think?" Ben asked. "How about your scary version of Chaucer or Boccaccio?"

"Actually, there was one story that I didn't base on any of the classics. I made it up myself. It was my masterpiece. The kids really loved it. It became so popular that they'd ask me to tell it again and again, and they would even retell it to the kids from other units. I heard that it became sort of a camp legend, and the kids were telling it to each other long after I left."

"Wow! It's not too terrifying, though? I won't be scarred for life?"

"I can't guarantee you that, but if you are, it's going to be worth it."

"Okay, go."

Lena peered into the flames and cleared her throat.

"Once upon a time, two girls went to fetch a pail of water. One was blond and fat, the other dark-haired and skinny, and neither of them was very pretty."

Ben chuckled. Lena smiled too: "I don't know why, but this line about the girls not being pretty always managed to crack the kids up. Okay, so. Both girls were wearing summer dresses, sandals, and white socks. They didn't have a pail, so each of them carried a large tin teakettle. There was plenty of drinking water in the camp, but it didn't taste good. People fetched water from the little spring that ran under the trees just off the road a couple of miles away from the camp. The two girls went out the gate and started to walk down the country road. There were almost no cars on the road. Just one or two passed by. It was a long walk. By the time they got to the spring, the sun had dropped to the tops of the trees in the woods and become heavy and large and red, and then it fell behind the clouds. They stepped off the road and walked up to the spring and then took turns filling their teakettles. 'Look!' the skinny girl said when they made it back to the road. 'What?' the fat girl asked. The skinny girl pointed to the sky. There was a huge fiery disc in the sky, just above the top line of woods. It was about three times as big as the sun and it was moving. Going up and down. Slowly. It would drop and graze the tops of trees and then rise a little, drop and rise again. The thin girl was so stunned that she splashed some water over her dress.

" 'Do you know what that is?' the fat girl asked her.

" 'The sun?' the thin girl answered.

" 'Does it look like the sun? Can the sun move like that?' No, it didn't look like the sun. And they knew very well that the sun couldn't move like that.

" 'That's a UFO,' the fat girl said, 'an alien spaceship. Look, it's obviously trying to pick a place to land.' She put the teakettle down on the ground, straightened her shoulders, and raised her arms so that they formed a straight line. Then she closed her eyes.

"The thin girl closed her eyes too.

" 'Aliens!' the fat girl yelled. 'Here, right here!'

" 'Shh,' the thin girl said, 'they might hear you.'

"'I want them to hear me. Aliens! Come to me. I'm a space element. I'm a cosmic creature. I'm a part of the universe. Come to me! Take me.'

"The thin girl grasped the teakettle handle tighter as if it could help her to hold on to the Earth. 'Aliens, please, please, don't come,' she whispered, 'or if you come, don't take me, take Inka, she really wants you to take her. I don't. She is a cosmic creature. I'm not.'"

Ben laughed.

"The kids would start laughing too," Lena said, "and sometimes they would even chant: 'Take Inka! Take Inka.'

"They felt a sharp gust of wind. Then another.

"The fat girl opened her eyes. There wasn't a fiery disc in the sky anymore. 'Where did it go?' she asked the thin girl.

"'I don't know, I wasn't looking.'

"'Oh, shit! They're gone. We should've sung something.'

"'Sung?'

"'Yeah. Sometimes it works. But you have to hit a very low note.'

"'Oh.'

"And here the kids would always nod with approval," Lena said.

"The fat girl sighed and picked up her teakettle. They turned to go back. It was significantly darker now, and colder. The thin girl started to shiver in her wet dress. They'd walked no more than a hundred feet when a car appeared as if out of nowhere, passed them by, then came to a sharp stop a few feet ahead and started moving in reverse in their direction. There was a man in an officer's uniform behind the wheel. He stopped the car and climbed out. There was something strange about him, but the girls couldn't say what it was right away.

"'Hey, girls,' he said, 'where are you going at such an hour?'

"'We went to fetch some water,' the fat girl said. 'Now, we're going back to the camp.'

"'Oh, the camp,' the man said. 'I heard there was a summer camp around here, never been there.'

"'It's right over there,' the fat girl said.

"'Is that right? Do you need a lift?'

"'No, thank you,' the thin girl said.

" 'Are you sure? Those kettles look heavy.'

"The thin girl nodded, then shook her head.

"The man smiled, climbed back into his car, and drove away. Only then did the two girls realize what was so strange about the man. This wasn't a man at all. This was just a huge black sausage in an officer's uniform. It didn't have any legs, or arms, or head, and it was soft and wiggly.

"The End."

"Black sausage?" Ben said. "Black sausage?"

"Yeah, black sausage. The image worked wonders with the kids."

"It is a memorable image, I agree. As powerful as it is indecent."

"Indecent? How?"

"Black sausage? Come on!"

"Stop it! Nobody except for you has ever had dirty associations. Didn't you like the story?"

"I liked it. I did. It's weird, but it's good. It's just something bothers me about it."

"What?"

"I don't know."

Ben prodded the smoldering logs with a stick and cleared his throat.

"Black sausage . . ." Ben said, staring into the water.

"What about that sausage bothers you so much?"

"I don't know. I just can't shake the feeling that I've heard it before. I thought it reminded me of some folktale, but the part about the aliens is something else."

"I swear I made it up!"

"No, no, of course, I believe you."

"I mean, I didn't even have to make it up. The story is based on what really happened."

"What really happened? An alien black sausage came out of a car?"

"No. What happened was this. Inka and I went to the spring for water. On the way back we saw something bizarre in the sky. A fiery disc significantly larger than the sun and moving in a strange way. I guess it could've just been the sun, and it could've seemed to move because the clouds moved very fast that day. But we did think that it was an alien spaceship. You know, with all that talk of aliens in our camp, I was scared out of my mind. And Inka really wanted to have an encounter. Yes, she did beg them to take her. But then the sun went down, and we went back."

Ben prodded the burning logs with a stick and cleared his throat.

"But what about the car and the man in the officer's uniform?"

"That's true too, except that there was a real man in the car, and not a black sausage. The man was Major Vedeneev. He was coming back to the camp and he saw us on the road, stopped the car, and offered us a ride. Vedenej sat in the back. Behind the wheel, there was a new soldier. Grisha Klein. Inka perked up. He'd only appeared at the base a couple of days before that, and Vedenej had made him his designated driver. He always topped the speed limit and Vedenej loved him for that. Grisha Klein was a philosophy student who'd been expelled from Moscow University for his ideas, or so they said. He was short, thin, slouchy, with a long nose and wiry hair, jumpy and fidgety at all times. Inka thought that he looked like Pushkin. I thought that he looked like a blinking, crackling lightbulb. Inka hurried to climb into the passenger's seat next to Grisha. I had to climb into the back seat, careful not to splash my water. I thought Inka would start talking about our extraterrestrial encounter, but she kept silent. She just kept looking at Grisha, trying to catch his gaze. Grisha was staring straight ahead, whistling a weird potpourri of opera and underground Russian rock. His right knee trembled and shook really hard. The car kept jumping up and down, and I thought this was not because the road was bumpy, but because of the vibration created by Grisha's knee.

"'Your dress is wet,' Vedenej said. I said, 'I'm sorry,' and immediately thought that this was an idiotic thing to say.

"He pulled a white handkerchief out of his pocket, put it on my knees, pressed down with his palm, then moved his hand away. When we got out of the car, I saw that the handkerchief was stuck to my dress, I peeled it off and gave it to Vedenej. 'Thank you,' he said.

"'Vedenej has a crush on you—it's disgusting,' Inka said to me later that day."

"See?" Ben said.

"What?"

"Inka said Vedenej's crush on you is disgusting. Clearly, she had a crush on you herself."

"She didn't! You should've seen her looking at that boy, Grisha Klein!"

"I don't know. She could've used him as foil."

The blast of wind from the lake made Lena shiver.

She turned to Ben and said, "Let's go in."

"Go ahead," Ben said. "I'll be there in a second."

Inside the cabin, the smoky warmth came in patches. She would enter a cold area and then move to a warmer spot, just to lose it a moment later. The bathroom was the farthest away from the stove, so there it was almost unbearably cold. But the bed wasn't that warm either. Lena felt the chill on her feet as soon as she took off her shoes. She dove under the blanket to take the rest of her clothes off. She pulled her jeans off. Her sweater. She smiled because they were in fact his jeans and his sweater. She took her socks off. They were, of course, his socks, big and lumpy, the tips hanging over her toes.

She must have dozed off, because she woke up when she felt Ben's freezing limbs next to her. Poor Ben, she thought, and pulled him into the warmth.

"You didn't come this time either, did you?" he asked a few minutes later.

"No, I didn't."

"Fuck, I thought I'd last longer this time. I thought I'd dodge it, but no, it got me."

She laughed.

"What got you?"

"You know what! Coming."

"Oh."

"Okay. Let me rest a couple of minutes. And we'll do it again. And I promise it will be much better."

Lena yawned and turned onto her stomach.

"Or we could just go to sleep," she said.

"Really? Thank you," Ben murmured.

"Thank you?" "Really?" Lena thought, but a second later she was asleep.

Fifteen

The next morning Lena was the first to wake up. There was an uncertain pale light in the window. In contrast to last night, it was very warm in the room.

Lena wrapped herself in a towel and went outside. This would be the first time she saw the lake and the surrounding woods in the daylight, except that this was hardly daylight. Everything was damp and white, the grayish-white color of skim milk. Farther away, the fog was so thick that Lena felt the urge to reach and squeeze it with her hands or run her fingers through it. The sky and the lake were the same color, it was impossible to tell where one ended and the other began. She could see the vague contours of the pines behind the cottage, but nothing on the other shore. Nothing at all. No shore. No cellular reception. As if the life that she used to live had stopped or made a pause.

The water was very cold, she thought as she tested it with her toes, but she decided to plunge in anyway. She felt a shocking chill against her breasts, a cold current reaching between her legs, and pleasantly cool water rolling off her butt. "My butt must be the coolest part of my body," she thought quickly, and then she got used to the water and didn't think of the cold or her body anymore. Lena swam slowly and quietly in the direction of the sun, a pale yellow circle bobbing uncertainly behind the mist, too weak to break through the white. She felt disoriented and strangely happy.

She couldn't remember the last time she had felt this way. Well, actually she could. In the camp. In the camp's pool. Bobbing in the cold water, all mixed up and bewildered, and strangely, stupidly excited.

They had filled the pool with water a few days before Parents Day. Parents Day was a big deal. Apparently, some of the parents held pretty important positions at the Ministry, so Yanina went to great pains to make sure everything was perfect. She made the soldiers and the staff scrub everything. And she put the counselors in charge of a really complicated entertainment program that included games, contests, the kids' concert, and, of course, the pool.

Ironically, the heat wave had already passed by then, and the temperature wasn't even warm anymore, let alone hot. They were supposed to open the pool on Tuesday, but they didn't open it until Thursday, and even then they had a "soft opening" for counselors, staff, and older kids. She and Inka went while their kids were in the club watching the movie.

Nobody was swimming. The sun was securely stored behind the clouds, and the breeze was chilly if not very strong. And the smell wasn't that inviting either. The water was muddy-brown and stank of chlorine.

A few kids stood on the wooden walkway around the pool, shivering in their bathing suits, shying away from the water. Some would come closer to the edge and test the water with their toes and spring away. The girls were scrunching their noses and saying that the water smelled like poop and frogs. Counselors hadn't even changed into their bathing suits. They sat on the long bench on the right side of the pool and urged the kids to jump in. The soldiers who were still fixing things around the pool urged the counselors to set an example. Lena immediately noticed Danya in the back painting the pool fence dark blue. She hadn't seen him since that dance, but she had never been able to stop thinking about him. Seeing him made her both stirred and upset, but she decided it would be best to ignore him, and she immediately felt some discomfort, like a nagging toothache.

There wasn't space on the bench, so Inka and she sat on the plastic stools by the entrance.

The girl in the red bathing suit was the first to approach the water. Her bathing suit was a couple of sizes too small and kept riding up her butt, until one or another of her girlfriends would pull the rim of the suit back down. A boy in blue briefs ran up to her and splashed some water on her. Her girlfriends screamed something like "Yuck! Poop! Frogs!" The girl in the red suit jumped away from the boy. He wanted to splash her again. She started to run. He started to chase her. They were running around the pool. Then they were fighting and pushing each other into the water. And finally the girl was in. Thrashing with her arms and squealing like a piglet.

Inka laughed and prodded Lena with her elbow to remind her to laugh as well. Inka's excitement was heightened by the fact that her brand-new love interest, Grisha Klein, was at the pool, scrubbing a long wooden bench with two other soldiers. She kept looking in his direction, and even though he didn't seem to have noticed her, his mere presence made her want to laugh, shriek, and squeal.

Other girls started to run around the pool squealing, even though nobody was pushing or chasing them. But it didn't take too long for the boys to take the cue, and soon many girls were in the water. Some girls would slip and fall on the boards and the running boys would jump right over them. The cold and the smell of poop didn't seem to bother anybody anymore. The boy in blue briefs, who had started all this, ran up to the bunch of squealing girls and froze for a second while determining which one to pick, and then he turned away from them, ran up to the counselors' bench, grabbed Dena's hand, and before anybody could react, pushed her into the pool.

"I'm wearing my watch, you fucking idiot!" Dena yelled when she climbed out of the pool.

"My watch! You ruined my watch!" And she shook her wrist in the air. But nobody was interested in her watch; everybody was staring at her chest. At the dark contours of her breasts under her wet shirt, and at her nipples that looked as if she wasn't wearing anything at all and were sharp and long like erasers on the tips of pencils.

Dena followed our stares, gasped, screamed, covered her breasts, and started to laugh like crazy.

It was then the soldiers stopped what they had been doing and joined the game. Other soldiers started to chase the counselors. Most of the counselors jumped off the bench and were now running around the pool with the kids. The more practical of them removed their watches first and left them on the bench. Soon it was a stampede of people, big and small, dressed and undressed, boot-clad and barefoot. The boards creaked under all those feet.

Lena looked for Danya, but he was still in the back, still painting that fence.

"Come on! They're gonna get us here!" Inka screamed as she jumped off the chair and ran. She didn't run away from the pool, though, but rather toward the soldiers, closer to the action.

Lena stayed put.

"So we now have the pool, right?" Vedenej asked. He had this amazing skill of materializing out of nowhere and sneaking up on you.

Lena nodded.

Vedenej surveyed the scene.

"The kids are having fun?" He squinted at Lena as if unsure that he'd said the right thing, or that he'd grasped the situation correctly.

She nodded again.

And then Inka came out of the pool. She was spitting water, her hair was flat and sticking to her head, mascara smeared all over her face. But who cared? Everybody was staring at the wet moving mass of her chest. Grisha Klein dropped the wire brush he had been holding and stared at Inka's chest too. He looked spellbound, as if he'd never seen breasts before. It was love at first sight. Well, at first sight in the right direction.

Then somebody whistled. Other soldiers joined in. Inka squealed and ran to the bench. Vedenej finally looked at her. His eyes popped. Only then did he get what the fun was all about.

He chuckled, obviously unsure what the appropriate reaction would be. He wrinkled his forehead, trying to pick the right one out of a variety of different reactions. Then he chuckled again and looked at Lena with great determination.

Lena saw in his eyes that he was going to throw her into the pool, but she didn't believe it. Not Major Vedeneev! Not the camp director! She still couldn't believe it when he walked up to her, and when he leaned over, and when his hands were on her waist, and even when she was lifted in the air. All that time she'd thought that this was some kind of a joke and in the end he'd let her go. And then she broke through the pool surface with a great big splash, which she couldn't hear, and felt the deafening water closing above her head, and the cold, and then, when she emerged and took a deep breath, the smell of rotten frog poop all around her face.

Lena swam to the ladder and tried to grab the railings, but her hands were shaking from the shock and she couldn't get a good grip. She was just hanging there in the water when she saw Danya squatting by the edge of the pool. "Do you need help?" he asked, and the next instant she was in his arms. She remembered how enormous she felt after her first meeting with Danya. This time, she didn't feel enormous at all. She felt rescued for a second, but the next instant she felt very small, and helpless, and exposed, and she wanted to cry.

"Are you okay?" he asked Lena as she stood shivering by the edge of the pool. She nodded and ran to the bench to get a towel.

Inka was waiting for her there: "Look, somebody's in trouble!" she said. She pointed toward Yanina, who had appeared at the pool out of nowhere and was scolding her husband. But Lena didn't care. Her encounter with Danya was all she could think about.

She saw him later that day, during the kids' naptime, as she sat by her unit with a book.

"Hi," Danya said.

She said "hi" too.

"I wanted to check how you were doing," he said.

She said that she was fine.

He sat down across from her at the table. He wasn't saying anything. Lena wasn't saying anything either. She just kept opening and closing her book. They broke the silence at the same time. He said: "So how's camp life?" and she said: "So what've you been—"

He chuckled and said that he'd been busy at the base, but now Yanina had summoned him back to prepare stuff for the concert. Mostly drawing bunnies and hedgehogs.

He said he loved to draw people, but not animals, because all the animals in his drawings looked freeze-dried. Lena said that her favorite animal was a pig, but she'd never seen a piglet up close. He said that he'd seen many piglets, when he visited his grandmother in Ukraine, and told me how they ran around in packs, and how he tried to feed them carrots. Lena said that she used to imagine that icicles were magical crystal carrots that could grant you any wish. Danya said that he wanted to go to the Arts Academy, but they didn't accept him. He was planning to try again after his army term was over. Lena said that she was heartbroken that they didn't accept her into acting school. Danya said that his favorite novel was Heinlein's *Door into Summer*. Lena had never heard of it. He said there was this cat in the book who hated cold and snow, there were twelve doors in the house and the cat would go from one door to the next, hoping that at least one of them would open into summer.

There was something frantic about the way they talked. As if they felt that they must hurry, that it was absolutely necessary to spill all these things without wasting a second. But there was also a sense, not a sense but a vague prickly awareness, that the things that they said to each other didn't really matter, that underneath all that talking something else was going on between them, something far more important and urgent.

They both started when they heard the call for afternoon snack.

"Is it five?" Danya asked. "I have to get back."

"Okay," Lena said.

He looked at her as if he didn't know what to say next.

"You're not like other girls. I like that. I like you a lot." He reached over to hug her. His fingers were very strong, Lena could feel them pressing hard into her back. She turned up her face, and he kissed her with such giddy force that they swayed.

Lena was too stunned to feel anything during the kiss, but afterward whenever she evoked the sensation, it made her dizzy with desire.

"Tomorrow night, okay?" Danya said.

She agreed, without even asking what he meant.

And over the past couple of days, Lena thought, there was something similar in the way Ben and she talked. Not that the things they said to each other weren't important, but the fact that they were sharing them at all had more significance.

Lena's teeth started to chatter. She must have been swimming for a long time. She got out of the lake and ran to wrap herself in the towel.

When she got back to the cabin, Ben was already up and dressed. He sat crouched by the fire ring lighting a new fire for their breakfast. The air smelled of burning logs and oranges. The juicer lay on the grass by the fire ring, several halved oranges beside it on a paper towel.

"Hi!" she said.

He said: "Good morning. Get dressed, and get ready for the best breakfast you've ever had."

But when Lena returned, Ben was still struggling with the juicer.

"I don't know what's wrong with it—it's stuck."

He tried to pry it open with a knife, but it wouldn't yield.

"Oh, come on!" Ben said and, in a burst of energy, threw the thing into the lake.

"Ben!" Lena moved toward the lake as if she could somehow save it, but he put his hand on her arm. For a moment they both looked out in silence at the spot where it had disappeared beneath the surface.

"Yeah, just like that," he said, "a huge chunk of my past is gone."

Lena was sad for him, until she began to wonder if it wasn't such a bad idea to be getting rid of some cumbersome chunks of one's past.

They sliced the oranges and ate them like that. Then they toasted some bread over the fire, and ate it with butter and jam. Juice or no juice, Lena had to agree that this really was the best breakfast she had ever eaten.

Then they went for a walk along the path that crept around the lake.

The fog had finally lifted, and splashes of sunlight brought the woods into focus with painful intensity. The blue lake. The different shades of green on the opposite bank. The sharp white of the birch trunks. Silvery cobwebs quivering in the sun. The birch branch that bent over the lake in an arch. The clear water. The glistening boulders on the bottom.

The air became heavy, and it seemed like it was pressing down on their shoulders.

"It's going to rain," Lena said. "Don't you think it's going to rain?"

"I don't know."

They headed toward the north shore of the lake, where the woods were dense with pine trees. Tiny beads of water stuck to every single needle. The beads were not glittery at all, and not transparent, but milky, opaque. The air smelled like wet pines, like pines and lake, and in her mouth it tasted like pines and lake too, tangy and fresh.

Ben put his arms around her shoulders and held her close. He smelled just like the woods, though maybe it was his clothes, saturated with the smells of the cabin.

"Will you tell me about Danya?" Ben asked.

Lena started: "Danya? Why?"

"He was the third guy that disappeared, right?"

She said, "No, Sasha Simonov was the third."

"Sasha?"

"Yes, Sasha, the crazy little boy from my unit. The one that had vomiting fits."

"Oh, yeah, I remember."

"It happened during Parents Day."

Lena looked at the trunks of the pines. No two looked alike—she had never noticed that before. Some were pleated, some scaly, some cracked like dried soil, some stripped of bark, bald and yellow. So huge, so strong, yet strangely vulnerable, capable of feeling pain. They looked amazingly like the pines at the camp.

"Parents Day started with a frantic search for clean clothes.

"'You have to remember three things,' Yanina told us. 'Make the parents feel welcome, make sure they see that you care about their kids, and make the kids wear clean clothes.'

"Inka and I spent the whole morning rummaging in the kids' suitcases, digging through the clothes that, by this stage in the summer, were so dirty they stuck together, trying to find something that was at least moderately clean. Having made our choices, we had to scrub the dirty spots with our fingers. Inka was angry at Yanina for making us do it, but I didn't mind. I was going on a date with Danya later that night, and I was so nervous that I was grateful for any distraction.

"The kids didn't look much cleaner than their clothes. We debated whether we should make them take showers, but we decided it would be too much trouble, and anyway, if the parents wanted their kids to be clean, they shouldn't have sent them to summer camp. Before the parents arrived, we looked them over one last time and declared them fine. In any case, they looked much better than the kids from the adjacent unit, who had filled the empty crate with dirt and claimed that it was a sandbox.

"Of course, the first thing that the parents did was to try and scrub their kids clean. Most of them arrived on three buses at about the same time. They marched from the gates to the units, where the kids had been waiting like overexcited puppies. They hugged and kissed their squealing kids, and then, almost right away, the mothers knelt down and started cleaning them. In a pretty close reenactment of how we'd just spent our day, they rubbed the dirty spots on the kids' shirts between their fingers, tried to wipe their knees, or spit on their handkerchiefs and rub their faces. All the while throwing reproachful looks at us. And some of them even pulled clean shirts out of their bags and make the kids change right on the spot.

"After that we took the parents along with the kids on a tour of the grounds. We had been taught to introduce the buildings in a positive light. Like 'Our cafeteria, where they prepare all meals from scratch, all fresh and healthy.' Or 'This is our beautiful swimming pool, the kids will start swimming soon.' But the kids, of course, wouldn't let us talk. They wanted to be the ones to describe everything. 'This is where we eat, they give us cubes of butter on a plate, they never give us extra compote.' Or 'See this boy? It's Sasha Simonov—he puked all over me the other day!' or 'That's where UFOs land. Yes, they do. Yes, we've seen them! They hit one girl on the head, her brains oozed out of the hole!'

"Everybody was getting ready for the main activity of the day— stuffing the kids with food that the parents had brought. My eyes popped when I saw the parents open their bags and spread the contents on the picnic tables or, in some cases, right on the grass. Boiled eggs, salami, cheese, potatoes, pickles, pies, cakes, whole roasted chickens, canned meat, canned peaches, fresh peaches, cherries, watermelons, caviar, chocolate, and, of course, candy. Tons and tons of candy.

"As the tradition of our camp went, counselors were expected to sit down and eat something with each family, and at first, Inka and I were excited about the idea, but by our sixth or seventh roasted chicken leg and caviar sandwich, all we wanted was to lie down on the grass and fall asleep. But no, we had to eat more, and smile at the parents, and show them how much we loved their kids.

"Alesha Pevtcov, obviously nervous, took Inka's hand and walked her to his parents' table. His hair was combed to the right side and smoothed with either water or his mother's saliva. His parents looked just like him, and, in fact, remarkably like each other, both small and fair-haired, with pale eyes and colorless brows.

" 'This is my counselor,' Alesha said, and blushed. He looked as if he were introducing his bride. Alesha's mother looked Inka over just like somebody would look over a future daughter-in-law. It was clear she didn't approve of Inka's puffed up, multicolored hair.

"Myshka's parents, on the other hand, looked nothing like Myshka. They were squat and plump, extremely well fed and well groomed, just like prize pigs at the fair. They both beamed at me and kept thanking me for taking such wonderful care of their daughter. When I finally got up from their table, Myshka's mother gave me a five-pound box of chocolate candy.

"Around three we led everybody to the club for the concert. My kids sang the Pilots' Song. They wore dark shorts and skirts, and white T-shirts (distributed by Yanina). All the T-shirts turned out to be too big. I helped the kids adhere Danya's shoulder straps to their sleeves. The kids sang badly, but they looked so small and touching in those bulky T-shirts, with the beautiful golden stars on the blue background.

"And then it was time to say good-bye to the parents. Counselors who had older kids looked at Inka and me with pity.

" 'Good luck, girls,' Dena said.

" 'Why?' Inka asked.

" 'Didn't you go to summer camp as children?' Dena asked.

"We shook our heads.

" 'Then you'll see.'

"A big procession went to the gates. Parents with children, counselors who were going to take the children back to their units, and a few soldiers. Everybody was calm, subdued, a little tired, a little sluggish. Nobody was talking. We could hear birds and cicadas and the wind droning through the tips of the pines. But once the procession reached the gates, it was as if somebody flipped the channel, and a movie suddenly started, where everybody had a familiar role, which he or she played with varying degrees of sincerity and intensity. Teenage boys would successfully dodge their mothers' hugs and run off, teenage girls would soon run off too, but not before hugging and kissing their mothers. The smaller children clutched their parents, some getting ahold of the hem of their mothers' skirts, others hugging their fathers' legs, burying their faces in their stomachs, grabbing their hands. And as the parents tried to free themselves from their children's clutches, the crying began. By that time we were pretty much used to children crying, but we had never heard them all cry at the same time. Some sniveled, some sobbed, some wailed, some bawled, some howled, others made sounds that didn't seem human at all. Then the buses rolled to the gates and the parents looked at us and the other counselors with pleading expressions. We tried to reason with the children. And when that failed, we tried to take their hands, and yes, grab them by their waists and physically drag them away from their parents. When we finally gathered our children and brought them back to our unit, some still sniveling, others calm and energized, Inka said, 'It's kind of strange that Simonov didn't throw a tantrum.' I was kind of surprised too. And then we saw Sasha sitting on the porch of our unit with his back to the bushes. His face was tear-streaked, but he appeared to be calm. He was quietly showing his new set of expensive felt pens to another boy, whose parents hadn't come. 'Look,' Sasha said, 'it even has purple and azure and neon green. You need neon green if you want to draw real aliens.'

"A small woman with red puffy eyes sprung out from behind the bushes and ran toward the gates.

"Inka and I exchanged looks.

"'Isn't that Sasha's mom?' I whispered.

"'Oh, no,' Inka said. 'Oh, hell, oh, no, she didn't tell him she was leaving.'

"And sure enough, as soon as she was past the gate, Sasha sensed something. He jumped up, dropped his pens, and ran to the gates. We ran after him.

"He was too late. The buses had just driven away and one of the soldiers was locking the gates. Sasha stopped and looked at the road. You could still see the cloud of dust. Sasha just stood there not moving, not crying, not making a sound, until he doubled over and started to vomit.

"'Don't you just hate mothers?' Inka asked as we carried the listless Sasha back to our unit. I certainly did. I promised myself again that I was never going to become one.

"But that wasn't the worst of it. Now we had to raid the kids' nightstands and clear out all the food. Kids were allowed to eat in their parents' presence, but they were forbidden to keep any food afterward so that it wouldn't go bad. But of course, they tried to hide whatever they could. Just imagine the mess in their drawers! Broken boxes of chocolate, heaps of candy, bananas, banana peels, half-eaten salami sandwiches, half-eaten chicken drumsticks, squashed tomatoes, smoked fish mixed with crumbling pieces of cake. How they cried and begged us to leave them something! It wasn't even about the food, they must have felt that we were getting rid of the last vestiges of their parents' affection. The last nightstand was Sveta's. She stood in front of it and said, 'Don't you dare open that!' Inka tried to move past her. Sveta bit her on the hand. Inka screamed. She got so angry that she pushed Sveta onto her bed, and pinned her down. 'Hurry up while I'm holding her!' she yelled. I opened the drawer to scoop the contents into a garbage pail, but there was nothing there. 'Where is your stuff, Sveta?'

"'I hid it, you bitches,' she said, 'you're never going to find it,' and started to cry. And then it hit me. There was nothing to hide. Nobody had come to visit Sveta. We were so frenzied that day that we hadn't noticed.

"I motioned for Inka to leave Sveta alone and asked Sveta to come with me. I took her to my room, opened a drawer and took out the box of candy that Myshka's parents had given me. I took the top off and told Sveta to pick the most beautiful candy. I felt very good, very proud of my generosity and my pedagogical skills. She reached for the big truffle with a hazelnut on top, but then paused, raised her fist and smashed it into the middle of the box, making most of the candies scatter on the floor, after which she ran into the kids' bedroom and plopped onto her bed to sob. I wanted to run after her and say that I was sorry, ashamed that I'd thought I could fix it all with candy. But I was afraid to make it worse.

"All the kids had trouble falling asleep that night. They kept tossing and turning, and sniveling, and blowing their noses, but gradually for each of them the exhaustion defeated anxiety. Each of them, that is, except for Sasha. He just kept repeating what he always did, that he was afraid of 'where he was going when he fell asleep.' I told him he wasn't going anywhere, and that I knew this for sure because I came to check on them in the middle of the night and everybody was there, and he was there. I moved my chair up to his bed and he shifted forward and put his head on my knee. I sat and stroked his thin damp hair until his eyes closed and he fell asleep. I put his head back onto the pillow and left the room.

"I ran to my room, splashed my face with water, changed my shirt, and rushed out, hoping that I didn't smell of roasted chicken, smoked fish, or vomit. On the way out I heard Sasha calling for me again. I pretended not to hear him and ran down the stairs to meet Danya."

Lena was so engrossed in her story that she didn't notice the rain had started.

Raindrops, prickly and hard like grain, fell on the tree branches around them.

"Is it raining?"

"It's not that bad yet," Ben said, "but we better hurry."

But a few minutes later, the raindrops turned big and wet, and there were more and more of them, until they merged into strings, then columns, then a whole solid wall of rain. Ben grabbed her hand and they started to run along the path, jumping over tree roots and branches.

The path veered away from the lake, deeper into the woods, where everything had turned dark, sleek, and slippery. The boulders seemed to grow bigger, crowding the sides of the path, covered with soggy dripping moss. Behind the boulders ran the stream, filled with gurgling water the color of very strong tea.

"That's the little bridge," Ben said.

"*That's* the bridge?" Lena asked. The bridge was thin and delicate, half-broken, like a toy from a long-abandoned toy box. Most of the railing was missing, and the planks were broken in the middle, some hanging down, touching the water.

She stopped and looked at Ben. His hair was thin and dark and stuck to his head.

He stepped onto the bridge, turned to her and gave her his hand. She took his hand and followed him, trying to keep her feet wide apart so as not to step into the missing middle. She had almost made it, but then Ben lost his balance and pulled her after him, and they both fell into the greenish-black muck.

Sixteen

fterward, the whole cabin was filled with the sweet, sickly smell of burning wood and the moldy stench of wet clothes, which they had draped over every chair to dry. It covered the smell of sex.

They were sitting on the bed, naked, with a half-empty bottle of tequila on the bed between them.

"Did you?" Ben asked.

Lena nodded.

"You did? Really?"

She said, "Yes."

"But back there, at the Holiday Inn, you didn't come, right?"

"No."

"I feared as much. I have this problem that you might have noticed."

"What problem? I haven't noticed!"

"I mean, it used to be much worse. I used to come in seconds. Now I've learned how to dodge it."

Lena sat up tipsily and stroked his hair.

"Poor Ben. So what do you do to dodge it?"

"I try to hide from it."

"Hide? Where?"

"I imagine that I'm this tiny animal. Like a mouse. And I imagine that something big is chasing me. And since it's bigger and faster than me, and I can't run very far from it, I have to fool it, I have to hide in places, and confuse it. So I hide under a rock. In the bushes. Between the fences. But you know, more often than not, it fools me. I would dodge it, and get away, and leave it far behind, and think now I can relax a little, but there it would be waiting for me just around the corner."

"Ben! Really? Seriously? It's just the other way around for me! I feel like I'm chasing it the whole time, and it runs away from me, and hides from me, and it does exactly what you do—it dodges me!"

Now Ben turned to face her, his eyes giddy.

"Oh, I get it now!"

"What do you get?"

"Well, that first time, you had this really grave, really focused expression. I was worried that I was hurting you. Turns out you were just chasing orgasm."

"Stop laughing at me! I didn't laugh at you!"

"Yes you did!"

They drank some more tequila.

Ben shook his head: "Still, I don't get it."

"You don't get what?"

"Why female orgasm should be so challenging."

"It's not! Actually, I have a whole theory about orgasm," Lena said.

"Do you?"

"I do. The key is in continuity. It's like music."

"Really? How is it like music?"

"You don't remember what you felt before, but somehow your sensation at any given moment is partly formed or partly influenced by all the different sensations you experienced earlier."

"Uh-huh."

"I'm serious. Okay, so I've never thought about it like this before, but think about it! Maybe 'influenced' was the wrong word. Enriched? Enhanced? No, not enhanced. What I am trying to say is that a sensation at any given moment wouldn't be what it is without all the previous sensations."

"I used to think that solving the mystery of female orgasm was as futile as trying to invent a perpetuum mobile. But you seem to be on the verge of discovery."

Lena laughed and drank some more tequila. "I'll show it to you. I have this thing on my iPod."

She rummaged in her bag for a long time and finally pulled out an iPod covered in something that looked like cookie crumbs. She wiped the crumbs off and started going through the dial.

"Uh-huh, here it is. Chopin's Fantaisie. It's light and sweet. There is a timer on the iPod, so I'll tell you exactly when the most wonderful part comes."

She put on her headphones and took a pencil and a piece of paper.

"I think I got it!" she said, handing him the headphones and the piece of paper. "See, the wonderful part comes between thirty and forty seconds, then it goes away to return exactly at 3:35. Listen, so you can see what I mean. I'll tell you when it's time."

Ben put the headphones on. She pushed the play button and peered at the timer: 32 seconds. She tapped him on the shoulder: "Now!"

She peered at the dial again and said: "Okay, there the music kind of changed direction, went higher, got a little more intense, then calmed down again."

She tapped him on the shoulder: "It's coming again! Exactly three minutes later."

She pushed the stop button and took the headphones from Ben: "Did you get what I meant?"

"Yeah, I think so."

"Now, if people could only record and replay what they do. Record not just the actions but the sensations. Like this, with the timer. So we could return to a particular sensation and replay it at any time. The mystery of female orgasm would have been solved."

And she snapped the fingers on both of her hands.

"Just like that!" Ben said.

Lena reached for the blanket, but Ben stopped her: "No, don't cover yourself. I know what we have to do now!"

"What?"

"I want to draw you."

"Draw me?"

"Well, not exactly you—"

"Hey!"

Ben reached for the pencil and the piece of paper.

"I might be out of practice. I haven't done a picture of a pussy in ages. Not since working on that comic book with Gerry."

Lena laughed and moved away.

"No, no, don't close your legs."

Lena put her glass down and opened her legs a little.

"Great, remarkably beautiful."

"Really? Is it really?"

"Yep. It's fucking mind-blowing!"

She laughed.

"Lie down and spread your legs more."

She did.

"Okay. Here goes."

He made some bold, self-assured strokes.

"It's very challenging to show it on paper. It's all about the light. How do you show the curves? All about the light. Light, light, light."

He grabbed the bottle from the table and took several gulps.

She raised her head to look at his face. He looked completely serious.

"You know what, I'm not sure if my drawing is very good, but I think I caught the essence of your cunt. Its personality."

She spread her legs a little more. If somebody told Lena just three days before that she'd be doing something like that, she would never have believed it. She didn't know it was possible to be that intimate or that comfortable with a man. She didn't know it was possible to feel that good. And she wasn't even drunk anymore. Not really.

"Yes. Like that. Perfect."

Ben would glance up at his model, then drop his gaze back to the paper, the movements of his hands fast, confident, and precise. He crumpled the first piece of paper, saying that he'd gotten the proportions wrong, but then went back to work right away. He was especially thorough with shading, which he did with the "pillows" of his middle and index fingers.

"Shading is fun," he said, raising his eyes to her face. "It's as if I was stroking it with the tips of my fingers."

"Are you almost done? I want to see it!"

"Almost. Patience!"

The expression on Ben's face turned into one of studious concentration. He was putting on the finishing touches.

"Okay, ready," he said, and lifted up the drawing for her to see.

Lena squealed in delight.

"It's beautiful! Oh, it's so beautiful. And you know what, it does look like a hedgehog!"

"Does it?"

Ben took the drawing from her, studied it for some time, then pressed it against his cock.

Lena moaned. She wanted him like crazy, but what she wanted even more was for this drawing session to continue.

"Come here," he said.

"No!"

"Why?"

"I'll draw you first."

And then it was she sitting cross-legged, holding the notebook and the pencil, staring at him.

"I haven't drawn anything in ages. It's a nice pencil, though. Soft. I took this one art class in college. I turned out to be very bad at it. Okay, just put your arms behind your head. Perfect."

She put her index finger forward, squinted, and measured it against his cock. Then she held her finger horizontally and measured like that.

"I'm trying to remember how they taught us about proportions. I think you do it like this."

Lena shook her head and moved away to continue working on her drawing.

She was holding the pencil in the tips of her fingers very close to the paper. Ben was staring at her fingers fluttering over the contours of his cock in the drawing. She moistened her middle finger's tip and rubbed it against the paper to make the lines a little smudgy.

He moaned.

"It looks more realistic if you smudge," she explained.

She held the notebook in her hands and admired the drawing. She looked at his cock, then at the picture again.

"It's absolutely perfect."

"Can I look?"

She handed him the paper.

"Well, I'm not sure about the proportions—"

Lena threw a pencil at him: "Hey! It was done with love!"

"I can see that."

Then he pushed the drawings away, grabbed Lena by the ankles, pulled her right up to him, and said:

"Enough art talk, okay?"

His damp hair stuck out in all directions. His eyes were dark, bright, and happy.

"Okay!" she said, laughing.

Afterward, they fell asleep. When they woke up, a couple of hours later, it had gotten dark outside, and the fire had almost gone out, and they were no longer drunk.

"Is it still raining?" she asked.

"I don't know, I don't think so."

"I need to pee."

She put on his jeans and shirt, filled a mug with water, and ran out to the outhouse. The rain had stopped, and it wasn't that cold, but it was misty and windy, and not particularly welcoming outside. She peed, then washed herself as quickly as possible so that mosquitoes couldn't get to her. She couldn't really do it well, with just a mug in her hands, in the dark of the outhouse. How she longed for a warm bath! The first thing she would do when she got home would be to take a warm bath. This was a lovely thought, until she remembered that this would be tomorrow. She would get home tomorrow. In one day. In an instant she felt sober.

Ben had revived a fire in the stove and put the kettle and the big pasta pot on. When the pasta was ready, they emptied the whole jar of sauce onto it, and since they couldn't find a cheese grater, crumbled some cheese with a fork. After the pasta they had tea. And after tea they went back to bed. They both felt that this had been such a long day, and they were too exhausted, too drained of energy, to move, or even to sleep, so they just stayed like that in each other's arms. Listening to the rain fall onto the cabin's roof.

"Tell me the rest of the story," Ben asked.

The rest of the story. So this would be the rest of the story.

Lena sighed and started speaking in a soft voice.

"Where was I? Oh, I had just gone out to meet Danya. He was waiting for me at the picnic. When I came out, he stood up, grabbed my hands, and pulled me close. We kissed standing up for a very long time, and then he pulled me toward the woods.

"We walked to the spot where the barbed wire was trampled and broken. We passed the pool and headed onto the path that led to 'the end of the woods.'

"I was wearing sandals. The strap on the left one was broken, so I had to clench my toes to keep it in place. The soles were so thin that I could feel every tree root. Blades of grass and hemlock leaves brushed against my ankles, and the warm mushy ground sloshed against the back of my heels. I thought a garter snake might crawl over my foot at any moment. Or I imagined a squirrel jumping right onto my foot, scratching me with its tiny claws, brushing against my legs with its tail. I looked over at Danya to see if he was worried about the same thing, but Danya was wearing his black army boots. I had no idea what he was thinking about. He was silent, far away, despite walking next to me with a firm grasp on my hand. I stayed silent too.

"I couldn't believe how different the woods felt at night. We were walking down the same path that I had walked with the kids many times before, but I didn't recognize it at all. Without the visual markers, like that fallen tree or a certain blackberry bush, I lost my understanding of location and distance.

"The woods were quiet. No creepy noises. Whatever sounds we heard were so soft and unaggressive—the dull rumble of a plane far above, a rising rustle of wind in the trees, a mosquito buzzing—that they strangely seemed to be part of the general silence.

"Something small darted off a log and into the bushes. I shrieked. 'It's only a squirrel,' Danya said. I wanted to tell him about my phobia of squirrels. I wanted to tell him many things. I desperately wanted us to talk, because I was scared of what might happen if we didn't talk. I was much more scared of that than squirrels.

"And then we heard some distant shouting. Danya stopped and listened. 'It's coming from the camp,' he said.

"Back the way we'd come, I saw flickering lights in the distance, as if people were brandishing flashlights.

"I had a momentary ridiculous thought that all the commotion was because of Danya and me, and that they were coming for us. I looked at Danya in a panic.

"He said, 'Something happened, we should go back.'

"We ran most of the way, stumbling over the roots. I even fell once and cut my knee against a sharp rock.

"When we got closer to the camp, we could see that there were people with flashlights looking for something in the woods. I recognized Galina. I asked her what had happened, and she said, 'Some fucking kid ran away.' I asked her if she knew who, and she said that she didn't, but she thought it was one of the little ones.

"I turned to Danya.

"He said: 'I need to report to headquarters now. I'll be at the base tomorrow, but I'll come by the day after tomorrow, okay?' I nodded and ran to my unit.

"As I ran, I was becoming more and more sure that it was one of our kids. Sveta—she had always been a time bomb, or Sasha, or maybe Myshka.

"The first person that I saw was Inka, all disheveled, red-faced, and teary. She was screaming at the top of her lungs:

"'Lena!'

"'What?'

"'Sasha's missing.'

"'Sasha! For how long?'

"'I don't know. I went out for ten minutes, no more. I didn't even go very far. Grisha came here, and we just sat at the picnic table. And when I came back and checked on the kids, his bed was empty. It was an hour and a half ago. Where were you?'

"'I was with Danya!'

"'Danya? Why?'

"'Did you look inside? In the bathroom? In the closet?'

"'Of course I did, you idiot!'

"'In the cafeteria, in the headquarters?'

"'Yes, yes, they did, they checked everywhere. They sent Grisha down the main road in case the little shit decided to walk home to his mommy. They're even searching the woods.'

"'The pool?'

"'We checked the pool. Thank God nobody's in there.'

"I sat down on the bench and tried to think. I couldn't think of anything.

"'Let's just go to the woods,' Inka said.

"We ran to the clearing by the pool when we heard a weak high-pitched cry not so far away.

"We stopped and listened, but the cry stopped. And then it was hard to distinguish amid all the yelling and screaming around us.

"'Sasha?' Inka yelled.

"Nobody answered. We climbed over the wire and headed to the woods. Then we heard it again.

"'The phone booth!' Inka said.

"We rushed back to the phone booth. On the way there we heard the sound again. We were now sure that it was coming from the booth.

"We started yanking on the door, but it was locked from the inside. We heard another cry, high-pitched and pained.

"'Sasha, are you there?' I yelled.

"There was a pause. Then he said 'Lena?' in a tiny voice. Yes, it was Sasha.

"'Are you hurt? Can you open the door?'

"There was some scratching on the other side, and the door finally opened. Sasha sat in a corner of the booth, trembling. We pulled him out. He had wet his pants, but other than that he wasn't hurt.

"'What happened?' Inka yelled.

"'I went to call my mom. The operator told me to wait. I waited and waited, then I fell asleep. Then the aliens came.'

"His eyes were wide open, brimming with horror.

"'What are you talking about?'

"'There were bright lights and shouting by the pool.'

"'And you thought that was aliens?'

"'That was us looking for you, you little idiot!' Inka yelled.

"Sasha started to cry again, but this time it was relief.

"I took him back to the unit. And Inka ran to the headquarters to report that Sasha was okay.

"'I locked the door of the booth with a stick so the Black Sausage wouldn't get me. And I started to sing in a high-pitched voice, because aliens can't stand high-pitched noise,' Sasha told me on the way back.

"'You did a smart thing,' I said. 'If there were aliens, it would've helped.'

"I helped Sasha to change and get into bed, then went into my room and just slumped onto the bed in my clothes."

Lena sat up in bed and reached for a mug. Her throat was parched.

Ben got up and went to the stove.

"It's quite a striking image," Ben said, having poured water into the teakettle and put it on the stove.

"What image?"

"A terrified little boy in a phone booth. I can't shake the feeling that

I've seen it before. Doesn't it seem familiar? Anyway, what happened with you and Danya? Did you see him the next day?"

"No. Grisha came and said that Danya was being transferred someplace else. I kept asking him where and why, but he seemed reluctant to talk about Danya. Then I asked Grisha to give Danya my home address. He said that he would. Neither of us had paper or a pen. Grisha rummaged in his pockets and pulled out a piece of newspaper and a pencil. I scribbled my address on the margins. Grisha folded the piece of paper and put it back in the pocket of his pants.

"After he was gone, Inka said that she was certain that it was Vedenej who made the soldiers disappear."

"The camp director?" Ben asked.

"Yes."

"How did she know that?"

"She didn't. We just pieced all the information together."

The water in the kettle started to boil. Lena watched Ben take out two mugs, put the teabags in, and pour the water over them.

"Go on," Ben said.

"Well, Inka's theory was that Vedenej had a crush on me from the very beginning. That was why he loved to stop me and chat, and that was why he threw me into the pool, and that was why he was touching my legs in the car. Apparently, he was too scared of Yanina to act on it. But he couldn't tolerate other guys dating me either. So since he had the power to transfer soldiers to other bases, that's what he did. Anyway, we didn't have a chance to talk more about that, because I was fired the next day. For losing Sasha Simonov. Or rather for going off to the woods that night."

"Wow, I had no idea that's where this all ended. You were *fired*? But who took care of the kids?"

"Inka had to do it alone. But there were only a few days left until the end of the term."

"Did you stay in touch with her after camp?"

"I tried, but it was difficult. She found out that she was pregnant in the fall, and she married Grisha and got a leave of absence from our school. And after I left for the U.S., we lost touch."

"What about Danya? Did he ever write to you?"

Lena wrapped herself in a blanket and shook her head: "I'm sorry. I don't really want to talk about Danya."

Ben carried the steaming mugs over to the bed and said, "So you were a femme fatale after all."

"No. I don't think about it like that. I don't want to think about it like that. You know, it's pretty easy to accept that love hurts. It makes you feel so helpless, unprotected. But at least you're not to blame. It's harder to accept that you can hurt other people. That you might be responsible for the bad things that happen to them. You spend so much time feeling weak, knowing you can't make other people happy, and yet you also have this power to hurt people, and you can't do anything about it."

"Yes, I know. I know exactly what you mean."

Lena reached for her tea, but it was still very hot, so she just blew on her mug.

Lena turned to her side and ran her hand against the wall. Chipped, splintery wood, rough against her fingers. A drop of water fell on her cheek. She wiped it off. Then another drop of water. She sat up and turned her face up.

"What?" Ben asked.

Another drop fell.

"The ceiling's leaking!"

Ben stood up in bed and reached for the boards in the ceiling.

"Fuck!"

He looked very funny like that. A little awkward. It always seemed to Lena that naked men looked more awkward and more exposed than naked women. His penis drooping to the right side, dark and delicate. She was suddenly flooded with so much affection for Ben that it made it hard to breathe. She couldn't remember when she had ever felt that way about Vadim.

Ben found the hole between the boards and closed it with his finger.

"Are you going to stand like that forever?" she asked.

"Um. Maybe. You know what? Hand me a piece of bread."

She got off the bed and broke off a piece of baguette.

"Smaller than that. And no crust, please."

Lena tore out a soft piece from the middle. Ben stuck it into the hole and waited. There were no more drops.

"Let's hope for the best," he said, and climbed back into bed. Lena gave him his mug and snuggled against his shoulder.

"Listen, that image of a little boy in the phone booth—" Ben said.

"Sasha?"

"Yes. I'm positive I've seen it somewhere."

"Where?"

"Wait, let me think."

He put his mug down and covered his face with his hands. Then he dropped his hands and looked at Lena.

"I think I know where. I bought this graphic novel about five years ago. It was published somewhere in Europe. London, I think. It was about a Soviet summer camp. A mildly pornographic horror story. Some of the art was amazing, but overall I don't think it was very good. I'm pretty sure there was the same crazy shit about that black sausage of yours. Only it was called purple sausage and it was drawn as a cock."

Lena's heart was thumping like crazy. Could it be that there was a book about her summer camp out there? A real, published book?

Lena sat up in bed and clutched the edge of the blanket: "I have to see it! Do you have it here?"

"I might. Leslie packed up most of my graphic novels, except for the ones I need for my class and a few famous ones. And since that one wasn't famous and I never used it for my teaching, there is a very good chance that I have it here."

"Look for it! Please, look for it!"

"Yes, sure."

They climbed out of the bed, put on their clothes, and went over to the cold corner of the cabin where Ben had dumped the boxes.

There were hundreds of books, mostly old, yellowed, well worn, with greasy pages, but some of them new.

"What does it look like?" Lena asked. "Is it big? Small? Hardcover?"

"I think it was softcover, but rather large. Dark cover."

Lena had two fears. First, that they wouldn't find the book at all. And second, that they'd find it but it wouldn't have anything to do with her camp or her story. That this would be just some weird coincidence.

"Here it is!" Ben said, holding up an oversized album in a dark brown cover. He carried it back to the bed.

Lena felt a terrible surge of nausea. She wished now it wouldn't have anything to do with her camp or her story. She was terrified of whatever they might find.

Ben plopped onto the bed with the book.

"Yep. *Hands over the Blankets*—just as I remembered. Okay. Now, who is the author? Simon Alexander. Does that ring a bell?"

Lena shook her head. No, she didn't know anybody by that name. She walked to the bed and sat down on the edge next to Ben.

"How about his photo?"

A gloomy-looking man in his late twenties or early thirties. Glasses. Thinning hair.

She shook her head again. Perhaps this was only a coincidence.

"Let's look at his bio," Ben said.

"Simon Alexander grew up in Moscow, Russia. He lives in London and works at . . . *Hands over the Blankets* is his first book."

London? Was this book that "amazing thing" that Sveta Kozlova wanted to show to her? And Inka? Inka mentioned that she'd met up with Sveta Kozlova.

The description claimed that this was one of the most striking debuts of recent years and one of the most "haunting stories of sexual oppression," where "a melodrama of first innocent love unfurled through mad jealousy and escalated to a dizzying climax," where it ended "in sabotage, shame, and despair," but was somehow told with "delightful humor."

"Should we read it?" Ben asked.

Lena took the book from him and opened it in her lap. On page 1 there was a whole-page drawing of a little boy caught masturbating. The caption read: *"They would storm into our room at night and yell: 'Hands over the blankets!' "*

The drawing was pretty realistic—tiny limp penis squeezed in the child's hands. There was horror in the child's eyes.

Lena recognized those eyes.

"Sasha Simonov?"

Lena closed the book and peered into the author's photo. She could now see some resemblance. Sasha who'd always wanted to become an artist. His full name was Alexander Simonov. He simply switched his last and first names to make his alias. How did he end up in London? But then so many people had left Russia, it was probably easier to meet some old acquaintance abroad. Anyway, none of it mattered.

"Yes, that was him. That's not true, though," Lena said.

"What's not true?"

"We never yelled anything like that."

"Well, perhaps, this was his artist's imagination at work."

Lena turned to the next page. The whole page looked like a tribute to the idyll of Sasha's family life. His father was in the center as a framed portrait. Large and square, he looked nothing like Sasha. He was wearing a military uniform with huge golden stars on his shoulder straps.

"Is he supposed to be a general or something?" Ben asked.

"I don't know. But I guess he must have been a big shot. I had no idea."

Sasha's mother was a pretty petite thing sitting in an armchair next to the portrait. Sasha, himself, was a tiny faceless figure by her feet. The family belongings took up the rest of the space in the drawing. There was a huge TV, a cabinet with gleaming porcelain, an enormous stereo system, and an opened fridge with a pineapple and a bunch of bananas as a centerpiece, and several jars on different shelves, each labeled CAVIAR.

"Yep, the dad must have been a big shot," Lena said.

"We were a happy family. We owned things nobody's even dreamed of," the caption read.

The next frame featured the same room with the portrait, armchair, and fridge filled with caviar. But the mom was drawn tiptoeing out of the apartment with a suitcase, where a man in a hat was waiting for her, and the dad in the portrait looked forlorn and lost.

"They thought summer camp would be a nice distraction. Or perhaps they were too busy to deal with me," the next caption said.

There was a ramshackle bus in the center going down the dusty road. Sasha was in the back of the bus. Looking out onto the road. Crying.

The next series of frames depicted the kids' daily activities at the camp. Morning assembly. Meals. Playtime. Bathroom. All of these frames showed ugly screaming women and kids looking terrified.

"The days were filled with horrors, big and small."

On the next page was a close-up of one of the horrors. A little boy, who looked like the masturbating boy from the first drawing, made some kind of a mess in the cafeteria, and the woman with huge boobs and teeth was yelling at him. And in the next frame the boy was throwing up. Supposedly from horror.

"As were the nights."

The next page was done as a series of four frames. A boys' bedroom in sinister moonlight in each of them. The boys lying in bed. Hands above the blankets. A woman sitting on the windowsill with speech bubbles coming off her face—apparently telling the kids a story.

"And then he took her to the woods."

Sasha's face stricken with horror.

"And then he tied her to the tree."

Sasha's face stricken with horror. A small bright yellow spot on his bed.

"And then he killed her."

The yellow spot spreading over the bed.

"And then he ate her."

Sasha's bed turned into an enormous yellow puddle. He is drowning there.

"That wasn't true!" Lena said. "Our stories weren't that scary!"

The other kids in the drawings looked pretty scary as well. Most of them had murderous expressions. And the games that they played all appeared to be pretty violent.

"Brueghel," Ben said. "Don't you see the resemblance?"

"I don't know, kind of," Lena said.

"This boy managed to pull it off."

In some of the pictures Sasha was drawn next to a husky little girl, about twice his size.

"Sveta was my only friend."

"She would protect me from other kids." (Sveta drawn pounding on some vicious-looking boys.)

"But more often than not she would beat me up herself."

(Sveta pounding on Sasha.)

The following page was flooded with blue light. There was a teenage girl in the center, with dark messy hair and huge anime eyes stroking the crying Sasha on the head. The boy was smiling, even though his clothes were covered in vomit.

"Her name was Lena," the caption said. *"It was love at first sight."*

"Is that you?" Ben asked. "Was he in love with you?"

"Oh my God. He was ten!" Lena said.

"I would've fallen in love with you when I was ten."

Next there was a long and rather boring series of frames depicting a walk in the woods. Lena skimmed through, until a page-sized rendition of a hedgehog made her stop. The boy was holding the hedgehog in his outstretched hands, about to give it to Lena. But Lena declined the gift.

"It can't be kept captive," she said. *"It will die of boredom and gloom."*

The eyes of the hedgehog were actually clouded with sadness. Lena had never seen anything like that.

"Amazing drawing, isn't it?" Ben asked. He was right next to her. Exuding heat and the smell of campfire smoke. His hand on her shoulder. Studying the drawings at the same time as she was. It felt very intimate. Perhaps too intimate.

The next frame was almost entirely dark, with the barely distinguishable silhouette of Lena hovering over the boy's bed.

"Every night, I waited for her to come and sit by my bed."

"Do you think Inka meant Sasha? Was he your secret admirer?" Ben asked.

"I don't know. I never thought of him that way," Lena said. She thought of Inka's expression. She said "secret admirer" with a smirk. She must have seen the book. She must have meant Sasha.

"Every night the counselors would go on dates with soldiers. Lena was the only one that stayed with us. I hoped and prayed it would always be this way. It wasn't."

There was a drawing of a dark camp unit seen from outside. The lonely figure of Lena by the window.

The next frame was flooded with colors and light. It showed a dance floor in the middle with big waves coming off it to signify vibrations, and lyrics from different songs popping up here and there—one sillier than the next. Ugly figures were dancing, or rather contorting and twisting their bodies. Some of the kids were dancing as well. Sasha and Lena were standing by the fence. Holding hands. Looking on.

In the next frame Lena lets go of Sasha's hand and steps forward. She is dancing. Twisting her body at impossible angles. Close-up of Sasha standing alone, his eyes clouded with sadness just like those of the hedgehog.

The next frame depicted Lena standing by the picnic table holding hands with an ape-like guy in a soldier's uniform.

"The first one's name was Kostik. He was a moron."

The next frame was exactly the same with Kostik and Lena holding hands, except that Kostik was crossed out with two fat red lines.

"I wasn't going to take it."

Lena swallowed and looked at Ben. She had a hunch that something disturbing would be revealed in the next pages, and she didn't want to discover it in Ben's presence. She thought of suggesting they go to bed, and finishing the story alone after Ben was asleep. But Ben had already turned the page.

CASTOR OIL + LENA = THE RUNS
DATE + THE RUNS = DATE RUINED

Following the equation was a drawing of a jar with sour cherry jam with instructions on how to mix some castor oil into a jar of jam.

"Was that what happened?" Ben asked.

Lena tried to remember. She remembered Inka giving them sour cherry jam that she had snatched from the kids. Everybody except for Lena had some. Lena hadn't wanted any jam, because she had a toothache. They kept trying to persuade her to have some, but she was firm. Was it possible that Sasha could have poured castor oil into a jar of jam, and then made sure Inka "discovered" it? Yes, it was possible. Inka was famous for taking sweets from the kids. And then as she and Kostik went on that romantic walk to the phone booth, the castor oil started to work. No wonder Kostik acquired that tortured expression.

Lena looked at Ben: "But why did he disappear?"

"I don't know. He just shat his pants and didn't want you to notice?"

Lena laughed and shook her head: "Poor Kostik."

She turned to the next page and was shocked by its sudden burst of color—a bright blue with tiny golden stars sprinkled across the page.

The following picture showed Lena crying over the pile of misshapen shoulder straps.

"Here was my chance to make her notice me."

The next series of frames showed Sasha tiptoeing out of the bedroom at night, going downstairs, opening the envelope with the shoulder straps and setting to work.

"Sasha Simonov? *Sasha Simonov* was the one who made the stars for me? Not Danya, but Sasha?"

"Really? It was Sasha?" Ben asked.

"Apparently. There is no reason he would have made that up. And this makes much more sense too. I've wondered how Danya managed to sneak in at night to take the straps and then to bring them back."

She sighed and flipped to the next page. She felt embarrassed, disappointed, stupid, and even angry with Danya. Even though it was illogical, especially after all these years. He had never known about the straps. They had never, not once, discussed them. He didn't know that she thought he was the one who made them. He didn't know that she'd used them as a point of reference for all these years. Every time Lena had doubted Danya's feelings, she would tell herself to think of the straps.

"She didn't even thank me," Sasha complained in the next caption.

Lena thought of little Sasha doing that heroic deed for her, expecting a smile, praise, waiting anxiously for her to notice the straps, seeing how happy they made her, and finally being met with her perfect indifference.

"But I didn't know it was him," Lena said to Ben.

Ben nodded.

"I mean, even if I hadn't thought it was Danya, how would I know it was Sasha?"

"Well, he was probably the only one in your unit who was good at art."

"That's true. He was."

Lena sighed and turned the page.

The following frames told the story of Vasyok stealing salami to win Lena's heart and Sasha spying on him, and then telling on Vasyok to Vedenej.

"What a little shit he was!" Lena said.

"He was mad at you for not acknowledging the stars."

"Still."

Lena shook her head in amazement. So it was Sasha who made both Kostik and Vasyok disappear. Vedenej had nothing to do with it. Was Danya's transfer to the North Sasha's doing as well? No, Sasha couldn't have possibly done that. But wasn't his dad a really big shot? Could it be that he asked his dad to transfer Danya?

On the next page there was a drawing of a thermometer showing 100 degrees followed by a series of rather uninspired frames depicting hardships of the heat wave at the camp. The only good drawings in those pages were the ones devoted to lambada. Apparently, it was Sasha's special talent to capture dance moves. His dancing Yanina was simply amazing. He drew her in such a way that she was getting brighter and larger compared to the other dancers in each frame.

"Is that Yanina?" Ben asked.

Lena said, "Yes."

"She's very attractive," Ben said. "I pictured her as this ugly old woman."

"She probably seemed old to me back then, but she was younger than we are now. Was she attractive? I don't know. She was red-faced and beefy—I couldn't see past that. And then I was so terrified of her that I mostly saw her as a monster."

"Well, Sasha clearly saw her as a very sexy woman. And, look, this soldier seems to be crazy about her."

There was a soldier next to Yanina in all the frames. He wasn't dancing, but just staring at her. Lena couldn't understand how she hadn't noticed that before. He had a beautiful, chiseled face and bright blue eyes. Startlingly blue eyes. He looked remarkably like Danya. But Lena didn't have time to ponder that, because Ben had already flipped to the next page.

"Whoa!" he said.

There were drawings of people engaged in every kind of sex and sexual position imaginable. Everything took place at night, outdoors, in the moonlight. All the couples were half-hidden behind the trees or bushes, but since there were more couples than appropriate vegetation, some trees gave shelter to two or three couples. Yanina had a whole tree to herself. To herself and her lover, a blue-eyed soldier. He wasn't Danya, was he? He couldn't have been Danya.

"Do you think he actually saw some of that or this comes purely from his imagination?" Ben asked.

"I don't know. I don't think he saw anything. The kids didn't really go out at night. I think it's based on rumors."

"And then the aliens came," the next caption read.

Ben seemed to be enthralled by the drawings of flying saucers and purple sausages, but Lena could hardly follow the narrative. She couldn't stop thinking of Danya and Yanina, and the more she thought about them, the more plausible the whole scenario became. Danya had an affair with Yanina. Vedenej found out about it and pulled some strings to transfer Danya to the North. It made sense. It made much more sense than her own idiotic femme fatale theory. She had nothing to do with Danya's transfer. She wasn't a femme fatale. She wasn't a romantic heroine. Well, she was, but only in her own dreams and the fantasies of a ten-year-old boy.

"Wait, who is that?" Ben asked.

There was a drawing of Lena talking to the blue-eyed soldier outside of the unit. They were holding hands. Lena was smiling and trembling. She was actually drawn in trembling motion lines. And Sasha was right there watching the scene with a bleeding heart. The heart was drawn over Sasha's white T-shirt, dripping blood.

"Isn't that the same guy who was with Yanina?"

Lena stared at the drawing in silence.

Ben took her hands in his and asked, "Is that Danya?"

She said, "Yes. Yes . . . This is Danya. I had no idea."

She freed her hands, took the book from Ben, and flipped through the rest. A series of frames about Parents Day, the detailed story of Sasha's disappearance, Lena's departure, Sasha's guilt when he found out that she was fired because of him, Sasha's grief. The last picture depicted a sobbing little boy drawing a hedgehog in shaky lines.

Lena shut the book. So that was how it was. The only one who had truly loved her was the little boy, Sasha. Danya didn't love her. Not then, not at the camp. He was attracted to her. He liked her. He loved talking to her. But it was Yanina he was crazy about. The awful Yanina. If he were to tell his own story about their camp, Lena would have been just a minor character. She didn't know if that newfound knowledge changed anything for her, but it hurt. It hurt a lot.

She started to cry.

Ben took her into his arms and stroked her back with such tenderness that it made her cry harder.

"Do you think that was how it happened?" he asked.

"Yes, I'm sure that was how it happened. Sasha might be wrong about small details, but everything else adds up."

Her face was pressed into his chest, so her words came out muffled.

She had felt awkward about reading the book with Ben, but now she was deeply moved by the fact that Ben was there with her as she was learning what really happened in her camp story. She had told him her version, but they had discovered the real version together. It was he who gave her the book, the book that had been in his car the whole time they were driving to Maine, hidden between the pieces of Ben's past, witness to everything that happened between them, and to Lena's delusional interpretation, the way those misunderstandings had affected the rest of her life.

He was so warm that she felt that if he continued to hug her, she would melt.

She raised her face and said, "I have to tell you about Danya now."

Ben nodded.

Lena took one of his hands and pressed it against her face.

"He did write to me. It took him six months. At first I was waiting for the letter like crazy. I would come down to the mailbox every morning and linger before opening it, prolonging the expectation that the letter would be there that day. Then I was hoping rather than waiting. Desperately hoping. Once, I even had a dream about getting the letter. And then I started to forget Danya. I thought of him less and less. There were days when I didn't think of him at all. Then there were weeks when I didn't think of him. After a while, I stopped thinking about him altogether. It was then that I finally got the letter. Danya wrote that he had been transferred to an outpost close to the Arctic Circle. He wrote that it was very cold and quiet there, but he'd gotten used to the cold very quickly, and he liked the quiet. He'd seen the Northern Lights, the most beautiful sight he had ever seen. The trees there were very low— knee high—and the animals were all white.

"He didn't ask me any questions. He didn't mention anything about the camp. He didn't say that he missed me. He signed it 'Danya.' Just 'Danya,' not 'your Danya' or 'love, Danya.' The whole letter was less than a page. I cried for an hour and wrote my reply. I wrote that I loved college, that I was studying ancient languages (we were supposed to study some Latin, but not until the next year), and that he must paint the Northern Lights, that it would be a shame if he didn't, that it was such a rare opportunity for an artist to see something like that. He didn't write me back."

"You never saw him again?" Ben asked.

"I saw him about four years after that. By pure accident. On a subway train in Moscow."

Lena took a few sips of tea. The story of her past was getting closer and closer to the present. Closing in on her.

"He called my name, and when I looked up from the book I was reading, I saw him standing right next to me. He was smiling. But he looked different. I wasn't sure how. Less boyish? I was so surprised to see him that I screamed, 'Danya!' He winced and said that he hated that name and that nobody called him that since the army."

Ben wanted to ask Lena something, but she ignored him and continued talking.

"We got off the subway together and went to have ice cream in a little café in the center. He said that he thought about me all the time, but he was too depressed to write. He said that being in the army, especially on that base up North, really screwed him up. He said that he got some very rough treatment on that base, but he wouldn't elaborate. Not then, not ever. No matter how much I begged him. I asked him about his art. He said that he'd quit art school and was studying math. He said that he thought that painting was stupid. We talked for an hour or so, and then I had to run to my class. He walked me to school. He acted like he was really happy to see me."

"Did you see each other again?"

"Yes, we did. We started to date."

"You and Danya dated?"

Lena cleared her throat. She had to tell Ben.

"Yeah, we dated for about a year. And then we got married."

Ben put his mug down and stared at Lena: "You married Danya?"

"Yes."

"What happened? Did you get divorced?"

"No, we're still married. Danya is my husband."

"But you said that your husband's name was something else. Vadim, was it?"

"Yes, his name is Vadim, which is how I think of him now. But Danya was his nickname."

Ben groaned and sank lower in bed: "Okay, I need to process that."

But Lena continued: "When we first got married, it was good. Fun. I loved making our home—it wasn't really a home, Vadim simply moved into my room in the apartment where I lived with my mother. But I loved helping him put his favorite posters up and set up his desk. And I loved shopping for food and cooking, and just watching TV together as we ate the pie I just learned how to bake. Vadim was teaching math to undergraduates. I graduated from college and found a job on the radio—I was in charge of finding and editing little-known fairy tales for a children's show. I loved that job. Then I found out that I was pregnant. Both Vadim and I were ecstatic. But soon after the baby was born, things started to turn sour. There was a huge wave of emigration, and most of our friends were planning to leave Russia to find jobs in Europe or the U.S. Vadim's parents left for California. Vadim eagerly supported them, saying that there was no future in Russia, for us, or for our son. He became obsessed with that idea, and whenever I tried to object, he would get very angry and bring up his experience in the army and say that I had no idea how horrible Russia was. He never really explained what happened to him on that base up North, but hinted that he had had a really hard time. And I kept thinking it was my fault that he ended up there."

"So you decided to go?"

"Yes. Vadim's parents were already living in California, so it made it easier to get our visas. Once we got here, we kind of switched roles. He became euphoric, and I became depressed. Misha was very young, so I was mostly stuck at home. I was overwhelmed by how much I hated everything here: from the sickening smell of eucalyptus in the air to the fact that you couldn't get anywhere without a car. But Vadim felt in sync with everything. He found a wonderful job within a month. He sang praises to the ocean, to the palm trees, to his new office, to the people around us, to life in general. And he didn't even notice how lost and unhappy I was. We were growing apart with such frightening speed. I would look at him and think: 'He is my husband. He's supposed to be the closest person in the world to me. Why don't I feel that way? Why? What's wrong with me?'

"Then I met Marcus. He was a graduate student in the film department and worked in a video store. He asked what I was looking for, and I explained how I had read the screenplays for all those famous movies, but never actually seen them and that I finally wanted to watch them. He found some of the movies for me and made me promise that I'd come and tell him about the experience of finally seeing them. We talked about movies a lot. And then gradually we fell to talking about other things. I don't even remember how it happened that we became lovers. It seemed to be the most natural thing in the world. And I didn't even feel horrible, because by that time I was so far away from Vadim that he seemed like a mere physical presence at the house, a roommate. I suspected that he felt the same way about me."

"How long were you and Marcus together?"

"For a year. He was the one that persuaded me to go to grad school. He wanted me to leave Vadim, but I couldn't make up my mind to do it. Mostly because of Misha. And then Vadim found out about us, and it was so horrible, you can't imagine how horrible it was. It wasn't just that he was jealous—he couldn't fathom how it was possible at all. I don't think he loved me anymore, but he trusted me completely, he thought of me as a part of him, you know, like an arm or a leg—he couldn't understand how I could betray him, the way he wouldn't be able to grasp if his arm or leg chose to betray him.

"I should've probably left Vadim back then, but he got really sick. He was sick for months. I got so scared that I broke off all contact with Marcus, I promised that I would never ever do something like that again, and I begged Vadim to forgive me. And then we hit that bubble of intimacy. Everything became brightly lit, brought into unbearably sharp focus. We were forced to see each other not just like partners or roommates, but like human beings with all this complicated shit inside.

We suddenly wanted to know each other, to understand each other. But what we found out about each other didn't help us in the long run; if anything, it made things worse. The most important thing that we understood was that we couldn't possibly understand each other. We were too different. In a few months I found out that I was pregnant with our second child. This time the news didn't make me happy. By then, whatever newfound intimacy we'd discovered had already evaporated. I felt further apart from Vadim than I'd ever felt."

"What happened to Marcus?"

"He quit the graduate program and left. I haven't heard from him since then."

They lay in each other's arms in silence, and then Ben said, "Remember, how you asked me if I was happy with Leslie?"

"Yes."

"And I started mumbling that nonsense about the elusive nature of happiness."

"Yes."

"I am not happy. I've been miserable for a very long time. But Leslie has this very precise, very beautiful model of happiness, and she builds our lives together according to it, and if something doesn't work, she just thinks of it as an obstacle that we should work through. In her opinion, family is something you have built and continue building, something that exists according to certain rules, something that will fall apart once the rules are broken. When we first started the affair, it was really intense. These little trips back and forth. Waiting, anticipation. And then, you know, the passion was gone, at least for me. But I was afraid to hurt Leslie's feelings, so I started faking it."

He turned onto his back and put his arms behind his head.

"If you stop and think about it, practically every single thing that we do is either to distract ourselves from what is wrong with our lives, or to please somebody else, to shield ourselves from reproaches and guilt. And while doing that, we're building a cocoon around ourselves, thicker and thicker, and we stay inside and suffer from loneliness, and long to break out of the cocoon. But as soon as we do break out, people around us get hurt, and we feel guilt, reproaches, and shame, and so we go back and continue building that cocoon, and it gets unbearably lonely in there."

"I know. I know. I know."

"About three years ago Leslie caught me with this woman I was seeing. Catherine, a sculptor. Leslie was devastated and she said that she was leaving me. And I was scared—you know, scared of winding up alone, yep, that's how pathetic I am—but mostly I was relieved. Because I knew that I didn't love Leslie anymore, and I knew that I didn't want to stay with her for the rest of my life. But Leslie didn't leave me. She went ahead and left her husband, so we could really be together."

"Are you going to stay with her for the rest of your life?"

"Don't say 'the rest of your life'! It fills me with such horror. The thought of marrying Leslie makes me sick, but the thought of leaving her makes me sick too. The process of leaving, I mean. I know that I'd be better off without her, and I'm pretty sure that she'd be better off without me. But I can't bear the thought of actually telling her that I want to leave. It's like a child's fear of throwing up. You know that in order to feel better you have to do something awful and scary, and you can't, you'd rather stay where you are and feel bad."

"Does Leslie know how unhappy you are?"

"No, I don't think so. For the most part, she doesn't. She has an enviable ability to believe what she wants to believe. And when she notices that I'm kind of down, she ascribes it to my general inclination to be depressed."

"Are you?"

"Am I what?"

"Depressed?"

"I don't know. Sometimes I get painfully aware that I've lived the active part of my life through, and from now on it'll be just gray and endless like the credits after a movie. Take travel. I used to love to travel. But now, as soon as we get to a new place, I have the acute sensation of a void, as if something essential is lacking. We appear to be fine, we talk, we laugh, we walk hand in hand, we do look as if we're enjoying the trip a lot, yet everything seems murky and distant, as if I were watching life passing by through the unwashed window of a train. And I catch myself thinking that I want this trip to be over as soon as possible. Leslie and I went to England this fall. Leslie was really looking forward to it. I was too, hoping for distraction, excitement, I don't know—fresh impressions. I tried so hard to make it a good trip, to enjoy it, to be happy. And you know what happens when you try hard to be happy. When you have to 'work' at it. On the outside, you succeed, everything looks fine. But inside, you feel such boredom and exhaustion. In one of the bed and breakfasts where we stayed, there was something wrong with the light switch in the bathroom. The light would go out every ten seconds or so, and then you had to fumble against the wall looking for the switch. I felt kind of like that throughout the trip. I would see something exciting—and I would come alive, and be pleased with myself that I was able to come alive at all. And then the light would go off, and all the things around me would look fake and dull like pictures in an old dusty coffee-table book, and all I felt would be boredom and longing to get somewhere else, to get out, to go to a different destination, to arrive somewhere where I could rest and stop forcing myself to feel alive."

"Oh, Ben. Ben. Ben. Ben."

The fire was almost out and the rain had stopped. It had gotten darker and colder in the cabin, and Lena became suddenly aware of the woods around them. Tall, dark, and eerie. Full of creepy sounds and smells. Lena turned to her side and moved closer to Ben, her hair touching his face, her ass grazing his stomach. She felt warm. Even her hair felt warm.

Ben hugged her and closed his eyes.

She shifted her body closer. He reached with his hand and touched her bare back, then ran his fingers down her spine to the little sweaty hollow. Her ass trembled under his hand. As they pushed toward each other, the position of their bodies on the bed changed, they seemed to be moving clockwise, until they were across the bed, her forehead pressed to the wall. She felt the fuzzy exposed logs against her face, splinters, soft hairy strings, the old homey smell of wood and decay.

She moved even closer to Ben so that every single spasm that rippled through her body reached his as well.

Afterward, she lay quietly with tears streaming down her face, down her right side, all the way to her ear. Ben kept wiping them away so that they wouldn't get inside her ear. He whispered "I love you" in an endlessly tender but barely discernible voice. She whispered "I love you" back.

They could hear each other's breathing, the sizzle of pine branches in the stove, and moths rustling over the lamp and banging against the glass. And then there were no more sounds, and no more images, just the heavy warmth all around them.

Seventeen

Lena woke up in the middle of the night with the strange feeling that there was a moose in the room. Standing between their bed and the wall, right next to her, pointing its head toward her, sniffing, and scratching the floor with one hoof. It was skinny just like the one they had seen on the road, with the same dingy, worn coat, and long strings of wet grass stuck to its chin. Lena knew that if she opened her eyes it would look right at her, and she knew that she should avoid that at any cost. "Why?" she thought. "I'm not the one who is afraid of moose." But she couldn't make herself open her eyes, so she just lay listening for the sounds the moose would make. The moose was quiet. At least it wasn't in distress. She hoped it would just quietly leave the room, but then realized that it wouldn't be able to do that. There wasn't enough space between the bed and the wall for it to turn around, and she wasn't sure if a moose could move backward. She'd never seen a moose moving backward. They probably couldn't do that, or weren't smart enough to figure out that they could. She snuggled up to Ben for protection.

When Lena woke up a couple of hours later, Ben was already up. She heard him open and close the door.

Lena started to pull on Ben's jeans, then remembered that she should leave them here. She reached for her bag and took out a T-shirt and her linen pants—all wrinkled, light blue, silly-looking. She got dressed, folded Ben's clothes, and put them back into the box. She picked the used tissues up off the floor and carried them to the tiny garbage pail that overflowed with the remnants of their food—they hadn't eaten that much. Two crumpled sheets of lined paper were stuck to the side of the pail. She knew what they were. The drawings they made the day before. Seeing them in the garbage pail stung. Which was ridiculous. What did she expect? That Ben would take them with him, frame them, and put them on the wall? She remembered the barely discernible words that they had whispered to each other right before they fell asleep. The memory formed a knot in the pit of her stomach.

She looked out the window and saw Ben splashing at the edge of the lake. He stood with his back to her. Naked—a towel, and a pile of clothes nearby on the grass. Shivering. Scrubbing himself with a tiny piece of soap. She put the kettle on, and took two Advil.

She was eating bread with cheese and drinking tea when he came back. She moved the second steaming mug toward him.

He sat down and started to drink his tea. He was still shivering. His long wet hair stuck to the sides of his head.

She finished her tea and went to rinse her mug.

"When do you plan to leave?" she asked.

"Soon, I think. Before traffic starts."

He put his mug into the sink and swept the crumbs off the table.

She wondered when the Advil would start working. He went behind the curtain and returned with the old thermos.

"Is there more hot water in the kettle?" he asked.

"Yeah, there's plenty."

"Do you mind making tea for the road?"

"Not at all."

She got the thermos out of the leather case, unscrewed the white plastic top, and pulled out the cork. The shiny surface on the inside was scratched and chipped. Not too badly though. She put two tea bags in, added some sugar—she had no idea if this would be too much or not enough—poured some hot water over the bags and put the cork back in.

"Do you want to take the book with you?" Ben asked.

Lena had thought about it. No, she didn't want to take the book with her. She certainly wasn't going to show it to Vadim, and she couldn't imagine that she would want to look at it again.

"If you're not taking it, I'd like to take it back with me," Ben said.

She realized that this was exactly what she wanted, for Ben to have it, for Ben to look at it from time to time.

She said, "Yes, please, take it with you."

He carried their bags to the car. That was it. She went out with the heavy thermos pressed to her chest. He locked the door and put the key into the little box under the porch.

They pulled out of the driveway onto the path leading through the woods. Lena kept turning back, looking at the cabin, once again marveling at its asymmetrical shape, and how lost and lonely it looked among all the pines and bushes. The car bounced up and down on the tree roots. She hit her shoulder against the door handle. She didn't remember the road being that bumpy.

The fog was lifting off the surface of the lake in patches. Where it had already cleared, the lake was a deep festive blue. And the sky was bright blue too. It was shaping up to be a really nice day.

When they drove onto the highway, their phones beeped to indicate that the wireless signal was back on. They were now officially getting back to their lives.

Lena checked her phone. There was just one text message, from Inka. She wrote to say that she was flying back to Moscow, that her plane was about to take off, but she was really hoping that they'd stay in touch. She wrote that she had been thinking about Lena these past four days. She promised to write her a long letter as soon as she got back. She sounded sincere, and Lena allowed herself to wonder if this time they really might stay in touch.

There were no calls from Vadim. It was still morning in San Diego.

They could be still asleep. Vadim in the upstairs bedroom painted butterscotch, with all those bright oil paintings on the walls, alone in that enormous white bed. Misha and Borya in twin beds in the downstairs bedroom. A tiny room facing the garden. She wondered if her mother-in-law's famous roses were in bloom now. She hoped not, she hated how they peeked inside the window, thorny branches scratching against the glass. Borya often had nightmares when he slept in strange places. She had an urge to hug her kids, to kiss them on the tops of their heads, to smell their hair.

There was little traffic, letting her forget about the road. She thought that she had never felt lonelier.

Lena looked at Ben's thermos in her lap. His old thermos in a ragged leather case. She had a vivid image of Ben as a child skiing with his dad. Freezing, exhausted, frightened, reaching for his cup of hot tea with gratitude. For some reason she imagined that he looked exactly like Sasha Simonov. He probably did look like him as a child. And even behaved like him. Ben used to be obsessed with death. Lena was sure that Ben used to be "afraid of where he was going when he fell asleep."

Then she had a vivid image of Ben fixing the leak the other night. The way he'd stretched and reached for the ceiling, and how he'd stood there looking at the drops as if counting them. Lena's deep and ever-growing affection for Ben had turned into a fleeting certainty that this wasn't over between them. It was unbearable to imagine that they wouldn't see each other again.

She put her left hand on the nape of his neck, pressed down with her fingers. Ben moaned and closed his eyes for a second before focusing again on the road. She dropped her hand and buried her head in his shoulder so that her hair touched his neck.

It was slowly getting foggy, as if somebody kept closing curtains over the road. One gray opaque curtain after another. Lena felt like peeling the curtains off, and she wanted to tell Ben that, but she didn't know how to put it into words.

"I'm afraid to fall asleep and wake up when we get there," she said.

She reached for a bottle of water under her seat and splashed some on her face.

"Ben."

"What?"

"Tell me a story."

"I don't really know any stories."

"Tell me something. Anything."

Drops of water were dripping down her forehead, all the way to her eyes, and farther down.

He scrunched his nose and ran his free hand through his hair.

"Have I ever told you how hedgehogs fuck?"

"No."

"Do you know how they fuck?"

"No, I don't."

"Weren't you ever interested in finding out?"

"Not really."

"Their backs are covered with spines, right?"

"Yes, so?"

"So, they can't do it the usual animal way, because the male can't get past the spines."

"Oh, right, right. How do they do it then?"

"They have their own special way."

"Hedgehogs' way?"

"Yes, hedgehogs' way. What they do is this. The female lies on her back."

"Can they even do that?"

"Do what?"

"Hedgehogs. Lie on their backs."

"Of course. They do it all the time. She picks a comfortable spot on the ground—a soft mossy patch is the best. She lies on her back and spreads her little hind legs as far apart as possible and she raises her front legs up. And the male comes and mounts her, but very gently. He doesn't really mount her but lies on top of her."

"But that's just missionary position."

"Yes, but in the animal world missionary position is considered the most sophisticated."

"Oh. Have you seen hedgehogs fuck many times?"

"Are you kidding? Hedgehogs are extremely private animals. Naturalists have to spend months waiting to catch them in the act. But I saw a video of them doing it three times. Once on the Discovery Channel, once on PBS, and once in an empty movie theater in the natural history museum in Springfield, Massachusetts. The whole act is very tender, because they do it ever so slowly and gently. One wrong move and a hedgehog gets hurt."

"I imagine that they rub against each other first. Their bellies are covered with very soft fur, and they get really warm when they rub against each other."

"Yes, you're absolutely right—they do that. But so lightly that you can barely notice they are moving at all. To the untrained eye they just lie on top of each other. But they rub, up and down and sideways until their genitals meet, and his dark hedgehog's knob enters her tiny pink hole."

"Pink? Is it really pink?"

"Why not?"

"Yes, you're right. Why not. Do they make any sounds?"

"Yes, yes, they do. They pant, and sniff, and grunt. Actually, I don't know if you can call it 'grunt'; maybe oink like pigs but not quite in the same way."

"Pigs are rude and they oink rudely."

"Hedgehogs are anything but rude. They oink very softly and tenderly."

"Yes, softly and tenderly. Did you know that every so often the female reaches with her little paws and strokes the male's snout?"

"No, I didn't."

"They didn't show it in the video?"

"No."

"Well, she does that. She strokes him. So very gently. She can't see his face, because her head is thrown back. She can't see anything, so it's very important for her to be able to touch him."

"Yes, yes. I know."

She fell asleep by the time the Boston skyline rose on the horizon. She sat awkwardly slumped in her seat, with her head leaning against the car door. He reached over with one hand, picked the sweater up off her lap, and carefully secured it between her neck and the door.

About the Author

Lara Vapnyar came to the United States from Russia in 1994 and started writing fiction in English in 2002. She is the author of the acclaimed novel *Memoirs of a Muse* and two collections of short stories, *There Are Jews in My House* and *Broccoli and Other Tales of Food and Love*. She is a recipient of a Guggenheim Fellowship, and the Goldberg Prize for Jewish Fiction. Her stories and essays have appeared in the *New Yorker*, the *New York Times*, *Harpers*, and the *New Republic*.

The Scent of Pine

by Lara Vapnyar

About This Guide

This reading group guide for *The Scent of Pine* includes an introduction, discussion questions, and ideas for enhancing your book club. The suggested questions are intended to help your reading group find new and interesting angles and topics for your discussion. We hope that these ideas will enrich your conversation and increase your enjoyment of the book.

Introduction

Though only thirty-eight, Lena finds herself in the grips of a midlife crisis. It seems impossible she will ever find happiness again. But then she strikes up a precarious friendship with Ben, a failed artist turned reluctant academic, who is just as lost as she is. They soon surprise themselves by embarking on an impulsive weekend adventure, uncharacteristically leaving their middle-aged responsibilities behind. On the way to Ben's remote cabin in Maine, Lena begins to talk, for the first time in her life, about the tumultuous summer she spent as a counselor in a Soviet children's camp twenty years earlier, when she was just discovering romance and her own sexuality. At a time when Russia itself was in turmoil, the once-placid world of the camp was equally unsettled, with unexplained disappearances and mysterious goings-on among the staff; Lena and her friend Inka were haunted by what they witnessed, or failed to witness, and by the fallout from those youthful relationships.

As Lena opens up to Ben about secrets she has long kept hidden, they begin to discover together not only the striking truths buried in her puzzling past, but also more immediate, passionate truths about the urgency of this short, stolen time they have together.

Beautifully told with Vapnyar's characteristic empathy and deadpan humor, *The Scent of Pine* is an unforgettable tale of longing, loneliness, and the relentless search for love.

Topics & Questions for Discussion

1. *The Scent of Pine* begins with a disclosure that at the Russian camp, "There were plenty of pines, and it was a summer with a lot of warm, bright days, so couldn't it have smelled nice at night? But it didn't. The smell was moldy and damp and a little putrid" (1). Why do you think Vapnyar has chosen to title her novel *The Scent of Pine* and to begin it with such a vivid description of the scent itself? What does the scent of pines signify to Lena and to Ben?

2. As soon as Lena tells Ben that no one attended her talk, "Strangely, she felt better" (22). Why is Lena willing to admit this to Ben but not to Vadim, her husband? When Lena lies to Vadim about the attendance of her lecture, she feels angry, "not with herself but with Vadim for some reason" (16). Why do you think she's angry at Vadim? Do you agree with her decision to lie to him?

3. What were your initial impressions of Ben? Why do you think that Lena asks Ben to take her to his cabin? Were you surprised by the impetuousness of the act? Why or why not? Why do you think that Ben agrees to take her?

4. Ben tells Lena, "Sometimes I think that the memories are better left behind" (89). Why do you think Ben feels this way? Do you agree with him? Lena revisits her memories by telling Ben about her summer working as a camp counselor. What effect does this have on her?

5. As Lena and Ben are driving, and she begins to feel comfortable in his car, she "realized that she was also starting to feel just as comfortable in the world of her story" (114). Throughout *The Scent of Pine*, the characters tell stories to each other. What do you think of the story Lena recounts to Ben of her summer at the Russian camp? Does it affect the way that they communicate and interact with each other? If so, how?

6. When Lena recounts her first date with Danya, she tells Ben, "I wanted to tell him many things. I desperately wanted us to talk, because I was scared of what might happen if we didn't talk" (151). Compare Lena's interactions with Danya to her interactions with Ben. How does she relate to both men? Were you surprised by what you learned about Danya?

7. Ben tells Lena that for Erica, his first wife, "Happiness was peace. Happiness was having a husband and a child" (91). How do Ben and Lena each define happiness? Does it influence their behavior with each other and with their respective partners? In what ways?

8. How does *Hands over the Blankets* help Lena understand her past? Where does the title come from? As Ben and Lena are reading the book together, he puts his hand on her shoulder, an action that "felt very intimate" to Lena, "perhaps too intimate" (160). Why do you think the gesture feels too personal to Lena? Has reading *Hands over the Blankets* together altered their relationship? If so, how?

9. At Ben's cabin, Lena feels "disoriented and strangely happy" and, when she tries to remember when she last had the same feeling, she realizes it was in the camp's pool, "bobbing in the cold water, all mixed up and bewildered, and strangely, stupidly excited" (130). In what ways is life at Ben's cabin similar to Lena's life at summer camp? Discuss what Lena's life is like in each of the locations. How does it compare with what you know about Lena's personal life? Why do you think both camp and Ben's cabin make her feel so happy?

10. When Lena runs into Inka in New York, Inka "seemed happy to see Lena, but there was no real warmth" (5). Are you surprised by this after learning more about their friendship? Why did Lena and Inka initially become friends? Lena tells Ben, "I'm insanely jealous of her career, but it's nothing compared to how jealous I felt when I thought that she was more popular than me in the camp" (40). Why do you think that's the case?

11. In describing the camp, Lena tells Ben, "Stealing was considered perfectly fine. Everybody stole. It would have seemed strange and even indecent if you didn't. But of course everybody stole on their own level" (80). Give examples of how people at the camp "stole on their own level." How was the camp a microcosm of what's happening in Russia at the time?

12. Lena says, "It's pretty easy to accept that love hurts. It makes you feel so helpless, unprotected. But at least you're not to blame. It's harder to accept that you can hurt other people. That you might be responsible for the bad things that happen to them" (155). In what ways has Lena been guilty of hurting others in matters of love? Are there other instances in *The Scent of Pine* where one character has been responsible for bad things happening to others? Discuss them. At one point during her storytelling, Lena and Ben joke that she is a femme fatale. In what ways could this be true?

Enhance Your Book Club

1. To gain insight into Vapnyar's writing process, read "Katania" (http://www.newyorker.com/fiction/features/2013/10/14/ 131014fi_fiction_vapnyar), which was published in *The New Yorker* in October 2013. Then read the article in *The New Yorker* in which Vapnyar answers questions about the short story: http:// www.newyorker.com/online/blogs/books/2013/10/this-week- in-fiction-lara-vapnyar.html.

2. At the conference, "Lena was suddenly seized by an acute feeling of being a stranger in America" (16). Discuss how Lena's life as an émigré has affected her. Then watch this video in which Lara Vapnyar discusses her own experience coming to the United States from Russia: http://www.youtube.com/watch?v=7a38OE4uUMs. Talk about how Lena's story is influenced by Vapnyar's own experiences.

3. When Lena begins to tell Ben about her time at summer camp, "She hadn't thought about how foreign her story might seem to him" (58). Visit http://englishrussia.com/2013/08/25/abandoned-summer-camps/ to see pictures of Russian summer camps. How do the images compare to the way you imagined the summer camp that Lena describes? Talk about your impressions with your book club.

4. As they prepare for a long drive to Ben's cabin, he tells Lena that he's looking forward to hearing more of her story during the car ride. He says, "It's like a welcome routine now. We go somewhere, we take a break from your story, then we come back to the car, and you start off where you stopped. I remember feeling like that when I was a child. I would be reading a book, a long attention-grabbing one . . . and I would have to leave . . . but I would be thinking of the book waiting for me at home" (94). Have you ever felt like that about a book while you're reading it? Compare books with the other members of your book club and consider making them selections for your next book club meeting.